CAN THIS
BE HAPPENING
AGAIN? . . .

We both sat on the flat rock near the creek's edge, and before I knew what was happening, Tony's arm was around me and I was pulled tightly against the familiar but frightening warmth of him. His hand gently touched the side of my face, turning my head toward him. Then, silently, sweetly, he kissed me. One side of me cried out, *No, don't let this happen;* the other side melted. I kissed Tony back.

Other Avon Flare Books by
Jane McFann

MAYBE BY THEN I'LL UNDERSTAND

One More Chance

Jane McFann

AN AVON FLARE BOOK

AVON BOOKS
A division of
The Hearst Corporation
105 Madison Avenue
New York, New York 10016

Copyright © 1988 by Jane McFann
Published by arrangement with the author
Library of Congress Catalog Card Number: 88-91509
ISBN: 0-380-75466-5
RL: 5.8

First Avon Flare Printing: August 1988

AVON FLARE TRADEMARK REG. U.S. PAT. OFF. AND IN OTHER COUNTRIES, MARCA REGISTRADA, HECHO EN U.S.A.

Printed in the U.S.A.

K-R 10 9 8 7 6 5 4 3 2 1

—To my parents, again, always

—To the nurses—especially Mela, Robin, and Pat—and the surgeons at Fawcett Memorial Hospital, for saving my father's life so that he could see this book

—And to Diane Crossan Sawyer, for unfailing friendship . . . and for all those walks

Chapter One

September came, as it always manages to do. I had gotten my hair cut, bought a new outfit, and was determined to have a good junior year. I figured if I looked better, acted more confident, pretended that I was no longer what Mary, my best friend, laughingly called a social reptile, just maybe I could pull it off. I had steeled myself for seeing Tony, the boy I fell in love with last year. I visualized him with every girl I could think of so it wouldn't seem like such a shock. I vowed that he wouldn't ruin my year, that I'd show him I was surviving without him.

In all honesty, I have to admit I wanted more than that. When Tony saw me, I wanted him to be just a little sorry that he was with Cyndee or Candy or whatever the flavor of the day was, and not with me. I wanted him to stand there, watching me stroll calmly, cooly by, and think, "Now I really screwed things up. If only I had a grip on all my problems, I could have kept Catherine, the one true love of my life. Perhaps if I turned over a new leaf, I could recapture that beautiful creature."

Right. So much for fantasies. Bulldozer Boy plowed right into my resolutions on the first day back. Literally, that is.

It was right before seventh period, the last class of the day. I was walking past the intersection of C and

D hallways, heading toward Spanish class. I had forgotten that there is a tradition in my school that the wall at that intersection is the Junior Wall. Heaven only knows how it started, but that particular stretch of wall is the territory of a group of junior boys who hang out there between classes, laughing, joking, yelling comments at passing girls, and getting chased away by the teachers whose rooms are nearby. There is another wall, located right across from the library, that is the Senior Wall, and any underclassman who values his life stays away from it. The same applies to freshmen and sophomores who dare linger at the Junior Wall. They have been stuffed into lockers, barricaded in bathrooms, and lifted up into the ceiling tiles. One unfortunate freshman made the dual mistake of standing at the Junior Wall *and* wearing sweatpants. Let's just say that he didn't look as good in his underwear as Jim Palmer does in those Jockey ads, and plenty of people had the chance to compare.

Anyway, I was approaching the Junior Wall, noticing the crew that had collected. Remember, this was only the first day of school, so the guys had to establish their membership early. Mark, Mary's on-again-off-again boyfriend, was there, along with seven or eight boys who I recognized but didn't know. They were part of the semi-jock/semi-prep group that was always popular around school.

I have to admit, though, that the final member of the group did surprise me. It was Tony. Now last year, Tony hung out on the smoking court, and he didn't seem to have any real friends except me. He was definitely a loner, more semi-hoodlum than semi-prep. This year, however, he had obviously chosen to join at least part of the junior crowd. He still looked like the old Tony, though. The concert T-shirt featured the Tom Petty/Bob Dylan tour, and the jeans were more faded than before. I even knew those sneakers, his favorite Nikes that I had once threatened to throw in the creek when he was teasing me one day in the park. Unfortunately, I thought he looked great, as good-looking and as sad as ever.

To give myself some credit, I checked all of this out in a split second. I don't know how, but I did. I didn't stop walking, or gawk, or blush bright red, and this was the first I'd seen Tony all day. My heart was at least up to my esophagus but it hadn't fallen out of my mouth, and I thought I was doing okay. After all, I had vowed to come back as a new and improved Cath.

Those were the thoughts I was immersed in, but I was still walking, head up, feet moving, arms clutching the stack of books teachers love to pass out to fill the time on the first day. Then, right at the corner, disaster struck—or make that Bulldozer Boy who struck. I honestly didn't know what hit me. What felt like a mobile brick wall rounded the corner and plowed into me. I didn't have a chance. I didn't have even a split second to avoid the collision. Before I could react, this hunched-over person clutching a mountain of books ran into me as if I were a tackling dummy in a football drill. I was down on the floor in a heap, and my books were all over creation, and all I could do was gasp for breath. I felt like throwing up. During the collision, his books had rammed my books straight into my stomach, and of course all of my teachers—and his—had issued hardcovers.

Quickly, I mastered breathing again. It was then, however, that I wanted to die. The Junior Wall guys. I could see their feet, hear their voices. "Hey, who the hell is that? What do you think you are, some kind of bulldozer? Hey Bulldozer Boy, we're talking to you. Get back here."

I lay quietly, trying to blend into the dirty school

carpet while also trying to figure out if all of my body parts were intact.

Mark leaned over me. His familiar face came into focus. "Are you okay, Cath?" I knew that he was trying to be nice, but that was a pretty stupid question. Sure, Mark, I'm fine. I thoroughly enjoy lying in the hallway, my books spread out over a twenty-foot radius, with what now appears to be a crowd of thousands staring at me, blocking traffic. Isn't that every high school girl's dream of the way to spend the first day of her junior year? A hand reached down to me, and I grabbed it and regained my feet. Once up, I looked to see whose hand I held. It was, of course, Tony's. He didn't let go. I know it sounds stupid, but one of the things I used to love to do with Tony was hold hands. He was good at it, he really was. This was not the ideal setting to resume that particular activity, however. Despite everything, I felt a tingle as his familiar fingers gripped mine. But escape was more important than tingling. I yanked my hand out of his, and turned to Mark. He seemed somewhat safer.

"Where are my books?" The voice was shaky and high-pitched. Of course, what could I expect under the circumstances, a sultry whisper? Mark began to gather my books from random watchers who had picked them up, and the crowd began to disperse. I guess they lost interest once they saw there was no blood or permanent injury. Call me cynical, but I know what kids like. Give them a good fight in the halls, and they'll gather around as if a thousand dollars was being raffled off.

I just wanted to escape. Tony was standing there staring at me, and I had the distinct feeling that some of the other guys were trying not to laugh. One guy's shoulders were shaking suspiciously. I suppose I *had* looked rather funny, but I wasn't in the mood to think

4

about that quite yet. The bell rang, and I walked away rather cautiously.

That was the start of my junior year. And that was my introduction to Robert Sullivan. He ran me down like a bulldozer and his name was changed forever. Bulldozer Boy—it came out of that collision, and it stuck. Boy, did it stick.

Chapter Two

Needless to say, I was curious about the person who had just caused me so much humiliation. I had a couple of theories. The first one was that he was a particularly bizarre freshman. After all, freshmen are new to the building, and they tend to be intimidated by the size of the school and the number of upperclassmen. Bulldozer Boy (already I thought of him that way) might just be more intimidated than most, and plowing through the hall with his head down could be his way of getting through the hallways quickly and into the relative safety of a teacher-guarded classroom. Besides, it made sense that he was a freshman, since I was sure that he hadn't been in the building last year. Even though there are a lot of students, even I would have noticed him at some point. After all, it had only taken one day this year.

My next theory was that he was a fanatical football player. Perhaps he lived and breathed to tackle unsuspecting victims—on or off the football field. Maybe he thought the football coach would see how quickly he downed me and give him a starting varsity position.

The only other theory I had time to figure out during my sixty-second walk to Spanish was that he was simply an inconsiderate jerk, in which case I certainly was going to give him a piece of my mind the next time I ran across him.

But the next surprise of the day found me suddenly speechless. There, sitting in the back corner of my Spanish class was none other than Bulldozer Boy. He, of course, was there on time, and I was late, which was definitely his fault. Anger raced through me, especially as I was becoming more and more aware of the assorted aches and pains that the collision had caused. My stomach was sore, the back of my head was knotted, my pride had definitely not recovered yet, and there he sat, big as life and not even out of breath. The Spanish teacher, Mr. Anderson, gave me a quick glare but spared me any lectures, probably because it was the first day and even people who had been in the building for years always claimed they couldn't find the room. If I were a teacher, I wouldn't want to hear that again either.

Anyway, all I could do at that point was to take a seat near the front where, of course, the only vacant seats were. I *did* glare at Bulldozer Boy on my way past, but he didn't notice. Come to think of it, the way he plowed into me he probably wouldn't even recognize my face, just my stomach.

Once I gathered my thoughts, I realized that my freshman theory was shot. After all, this was a third-year Spanish class, which meant it was filled with juniors and seniors. There was one excuse he couldn't use. Without being too terribly obvious, I turned around to look at the object of all my speculation. He certainly was . . . different. His hair was shaggy and uncombed, sticking up in random tufts. It was the thickest hair I'd ever seen, reminding me more of an animal's fur than human hair. It was beige—not blonde, not brown, but a weird shade of beige. It was the color I imagined lions were. His features were sort of big and soft. There were no angles in his face, no sharp edges to anything. His eyes were darting around

7

the room as if he were a secret service agent guarding the President. They were an unusual blue, almost a turquoise color. I don't think I've ever seen another living being with eyes quite that color, before or since. The rest of his body was hard to make out since it was smothered in a big, heavy, brown jacket. Now *that* was strange, since it was one of those wonderful September days when the temperature reaches about eighty degrees.

Mr. Anderson recaptured my attention since he was calling roll and giving out assigned seats. There were the normal groans from the kids around me since that meant they couldn't sit next to their friends. I had no close friends in the class, so it didn't really bother me. I heard my name, Catherine Berry, a name guaranteed to give me a front row seat, and sure enough I only had to move up and over one. From that point on, I watched the rest of the process. Name by name, students moved to the seat pointed out by the teacher. When he got to "Robert Sullivan," no one moved. He read the name twice, indicated the chair to be left vacant, and went on. When he had finished, Bulldozer Boy still sat in the back corner.

Mr. Anderson looked at Bulldozer Boy with a smile. "Am I missing your name on my class list?" he asked pleasantly. There was silence. Mr. Anderson walked back to Bulldozer Boy and stood right next to him. "Young man, what is your name? I don't seem to have you on the computer sheet." Still no answer. By this point, the entire class was paying close attention. After all, we were used to seeing kids mouth off in class, but silence was something new.

"I can't assign you a seat until I know who you are, now can I?" It was the last period of the day, and I could see Mr. Anderson's patience beginning to fray a little. The corners of his mouth tightened, and his eyebrows jerked up. Bulldozer Boy's eyes were no longer darting around; instead they were focused straight ahead. It seemed like he was looking directly past Mr. Anderson's right ear.

Mr. Anderson took another try. "Look, maybe you're not in the right class. Let me see your schedule." On the first day, every student is given a computer copy of his schedule, and we all hang on to them for dear life until we figure out where we're going. Bulldozer Boy didn't move a muscle. Now Mr. Anderson's foot was tapping. From my years of experience with teachers, a tapping foot is a very bad sign. Evidently Bulldozer Boy didn't pick up on that, however.

Mr. Anderson must have spied the corner of Bulldozer Boy's schedule sticking out of one of the books piled on the desk because suddenly he grabbed the paper. Bulldozer Boy lunged for the schedule, looking like he meant to rip it away from Mr. Anderson, but he wasn't fast enough. "Robert Sullivan," Mr. Anderson said, reading off the schedule. "Now why didn't you tell me that in the beginning and save me all this confusion?" The class snickered, relaxing now that the mystery was solved. "I'm going to assume you didn't hear me call your name. Your seat is that empty one in the middle of the third row." Mr. Anderson walked back to the front of the room, shaking his head.

Bulldozer Boy didn't move.

"Mr. Sullivan, your assigned seat, please." That's another teacher danger sign—calling a student Mr. or Miss.

Bulldozer Boy didn't even acknowledge that Mr. Anderson existed.

The class was getting interested again. I have to admit that I was riveted, too. Suddenly I had a new theory—maybe Bulldozer Boy was deaf. That didn't make a lot of sense, though. Wouldn't the counselors be sure to warn the teachers about something like that? I could see that Mr. Anderson wasn't making much more progress in figuring out the situation than I was. He was staring at Bulldozer Boy, eyebrows twitching, jaw twitching, hand twitching, foot tapping. After all, it was the first day of class, and he had to establish his authority or risk being considered a soft touch.

Mr. Anderson stormed back to the middle of the third row where the empty seat was. Dramatically, he lifted the desk several inches off the floor and dropped it. The crash resounded in the quiet classroom. Then, in a deep voice suited to a Shakespearean actor, he thundered, "*That*, Mr. Sullivan, is your assigned seat. NOW SIT IN IT."

Bulldozer Boy looked past Mr. Anderson's left ear this time.

With that, the bell rang, taking us all by surprise. After a full morning of assemblies and orientation meetings, our classes only met for fifteen minutes on the first day. There was almost a sigh of disappointment as everyone gathered up their belongings to leave. After all, it's not often you see a duel like that on the first day.

Bulldozer Boy was gone the split second the bell rang. I don't know how he gathered his books and got out of his seat that fast, but he was out the door before any of the rest of us even reacted. Mr. Anderson was saying "Mr. Sullivan, please stay after class" without the slightest chance of being heard by Bulldozer Boy.

He was gone. I sure didn't get in his way.

Chapter Three

When I got home from school that first day, I discovered even more damage from my collision with Bulldozer Boy. The back of my right elbow was beginning to turn an amazing shade of purple, and my ribs were definitely aching. On the whole, Bulldozer Boy certainly had created havoc, not only with me but with Mr. Anderson. Every time I thought about being sprawled on the floor of the hallway in front of the Junior Wall, I felt like switching schools. I sure was off to a good start convincing Tony that I was cool and composed—looking like a complete idiot wasn't exactly what I had in mind. I almost had to smile when I thought about Mr. Anderson, though. It's not that I wanted bad things to happen to him. I mean, I think I might want to be a teacher some day (if I can't be a writer, that is) and I don't sit in classes hoping to see teachers made miserable like some kids do. Still, I had to hand it to Bulldozer Boy in a way. I'd never seen anybody be so defiant in absolute silence.

I decided to be a dutiful daughter and start dinner for my mom. She's a lawyer, so she doesn't get home until 6:00 or so—on an early day. She started law school when I was twelve, which also happened to be when she and my father got divorced. Now she's doing really well at the biggest law firm in town. I'm proud of her, and now that I'm a little older, I don't mind her being at work for long hours as much as I used to. I understand that she needs her own life, and besides, she's been so happy lately. Mr. Donelly, who works for the same law firm, has been living with us for the past six months, and it's working out better than I thought it would. He was *supposed* to be staying with us for only a few weeks until his new apartment was ready, but somehow those weeks have stretched into months, and that apartment never gets mentioned any more—except by me when he gets on my nerves, and even then I'm really only joking. The last time I brought it up was when Mr. Donelly put a Julio Iglesias album on the stereo at 8:00 on a Saturday morning. He said it was just a joke, but I wasn't so sure. As soon as I brought up how nice that particular album would sound in his new apartment, old Julio disappeared. I figure if I've got the ammunition, it's nice to use it once in a while.

Anyway, dinner was not what you'd call conventional. All I could find in the refrigerator were carrots, celery, onions, green pepper, cheese, leftover chicken, and sour cream. We had some of those frozen pie crusts in the freezer, so I chopped up the vegetables and chicken, added sour cream and cheese, put it all in one pie crust, and sealed another pie crust over the top. Then I baked it in the oven for quite a while.

Mom and Mr. Donelly came in from the office embroiled in another one of their work discussions, but at least Mom remembered that school had started, so when we sat down for dinner she asked that question parents love so much: "How was school today, dear?" I'm sure she expected the usual "Fine, thanks. How was *your* day?" Imagine her surprise when I launched into a fifteen-minute reconstruction of the events of the day. At first she was upset when she heard how Bulldozer Boy had knocked me down, more than I realized she'd be, especially after I told her Tony had helped me to my feet. But I didn't want her to make such a big deal about it. And I knew she must have wondered about how it was for me to go back to school and see Tony again. I really didn't want to talk about him. So I wanted to talk about something other than school.

"Mom, it was the first day. Wait and see. I'm sure the school will take care of it." I changed the subject quickly. "How do you like the pie?"

Mom considered her words carefully before she answered my question. "Well, Cath, I really do appreciate your having dinner ready for us. You didn't have to do that, especially on your first day back to school."

I was laughing inside. If truth be told, the pie was really dreadful.

"But do you *like* it?" I wasn't going to let her off the hook.

"Well, Cath, I wouldn't want to have it every night, but it's a nice change." Mom was really sweating to find the right words.

Finally I started to laugh. "It's pretty lousy, isn't it?" I said. Mr. Donelly gave a muffled choke, and Mom started to laugh with me.

"Yes," she said. "I've had worse . . ."

"When?" Mr. Donelly interrupted. "Certainly not since you've known me."

I had to laugh. Mr. Donelly is sort of a snob about his abilities as a cook, but he sure had never served us anything as bad as this pie. To show you how bad it was, we threw away what was left of it. Now my mother is famous for saving leftovers, even the tiniest portion. Some get eaten, others grow green, blue, or purple mold, and one mystery food forgotten for months in a back corner of the refrigerator ate through the bottom of a Tupperware container. *That* one worried me.

The rest of the night was filled with phone calls. Imagine my surprise. There have been times when I haven't gotten one call in weeks except for Mary, of course, and here I got three in one night. They were important ones, too, especially the last two.

The first one was from Mary. She hadn't talked to me since lunch, and in Mary's life, amazing changes can take place in six or seven hours. This time, though, she just wanted to tell me about this boy in her sixth period class who had a great body and who she somehow just knew would be perfect for me. Mary, you see, has Mark *and* a waiting list of boys who want to take her out. Me, she worries about. Last year while I was dating Tony, she almost drove me crazy because at first she thought it was the event of the century that I had a boyfriend, but then she decided she didn't especially like Tony. I can admit now (even to her) that she was right about him, but at the time I thought Tony was pretty wonderful. I hadn't dated anyone else since Tony and I broke up last June, and she was getting worried again.

"What makes you think he's perfect for me?" I asked her.

"He just has a look about him," she replied.

"What kind of look?" I asked patiently. If you keep after her for long enough, Mary usually makes sense.

"Well, he seems kind of . . . sensitive," she said.

"What makes you think that? Did he say something in class? Do something?"

"No, he never said a word," Mary answered.

"And that makes him sensitive?" I asked in amazement.

"Sure," she said. "After all, some people show

they're not sensitive the minute they open their mouth.''

"Mary, he didn't . . .'' I stopped. I could sense that this line of questioning had nowhere good to go. Instead I told her about the collision. She was sympathetic, knowing how much I hate to be the center of attention. Now if this had happened to Mary, she somehow would have found a way to make it work to her advantage. She would have had herself dramatically carried off to the nurse's office in the arms of the captain of the football team or something.

Anyway, Mary soon decided she'd better call Mark, especially after I told her how nice he had been to me. She alternates between thinking he's a sweetheart and the jerk of the universe, and hearing he'd been practically trying to defend my honor made her decide he might deserve her.

I settled down on my bed, leafing through the books I'd gotten in school. The math book looked nightmarish, the English book looked wonderful, and the Spanish book looked . . . foreign. The phone rang again, and I went to answer it. After I said an automatic hello, expecting the call to be for Mom or Mr. Donelly, I heard that familiar yet totally unexpected voice.

"Hi, Catherine. I wanted to know if you were okay. That guy really leveled you in the hall today.''

It was Tony. He hadn't spoken to me and I hadn't spoken to him since the argument that had ended everything. Since it had been my decision, I hadn't expected him to ever call me. I fantasized about it plenty of times, but I really didn't expect it.

"Thanks, Tony.'' Notice he hadn't even identified himself. Notice I didn't have any trouble recognizing the voice.

"So are you okay?''

"Yes, I guess so. I have a few bruises and bumps, but nothing too serious."

An awkward silence descended. I couldn't think of a word in the world to say. What should I do, just casually say, "So how's life without me, Tony? How's Cyndee, or is it Candy?" I absolutely couldn't do that. It would look like I'd been checking up on him, or that I was jealous, or both. I wondered if he knew that I hadn't been out with anyone else. Why would he care? This was stupid.

Finally Tony broke the silence. "Some of us decided to find out about Bulldozer Boy's story tomorrow. He sure is weird. We'll talk to him and tell him to cool it with the plowing. You shouldn't have to worry about him again."

Now what was I supposed to say? Thank him for sounding all tough and macho? This was certainly a new side to Tony. Tell him that I didn't need him to solve my problems, that I'd handle them myself? That didn't seem very kind after he had made the effort to call me. Of course, while I sorted through all of this, there was another long silence.

"Thanks," was all I finally said.

"I'm glad you're okay. Goodbye, Catherine." Tony hung up.

I walked back to my room in a daze. What had I done? Had I just condemned Bulldozer Boy to life in a locker—or worse? Come to think of it, maybe that would slow him down a little. More importantly, though, just what did this call from Tony mean? He was glad I was okay. Was he glad because he still cared about me, or was he glad like he'd be glad no matter who the person was who had been knocked down? And *why* was I feeling this way? Why was my heart racing? Why was my stomach, already battered by Bulldozer Boy, now knotted up with tension? Tony was a boy who had given me great joy and great pain, and I was better off without him. I was almost ready to call Mary to get another one of her lectures about the evils of Tony when the phone rang again. I hadn't even made it back to my bedroom.

"Overseas call for either Angela or Catherine Berry," said the slightly garbled voice of an operator.

"This is Catherine Berry," I answered.

"One moment please."

The next thing I heard was my father's voice coming from Saudi Arabia, where he'd voluntarily transferred after he and my mom got divorced.

"Cath, how are you?"

I was *not* going to tell the Bulldozer Boy story again, especially at overseas rates, so I answered quickly. "Fine, Dad. How are you?"

"I've got great news for you. The company's transferring me back home. It's all rather sudden, but I'll be back for good in two weeks. It'll be wonderful to see you."

"Dad, that's great!" I'd only seen him twice in the past four years, the last time two years ago. We wrote to each other, and he called once in a while, but he sure hadn't been available for the everyday kinds of things.

"The details are already in the mail, but I couldn't wait to tell you. I'd better go. These calls are incredibly expensive. Be sure to tell your mother."

With that the connection ended. Phone rates were horrendous between here and Saudi Arabia, and I had gotten used to very quick calls that tended to end abruptly.

I went and told Mom. What surprised even me was that I wasn't jumping up and down for joy, and I wasn't even sure why. I had really missed my father, especially at the beginning. I had sort of gotten used to relying on my mother, though—or on myself. Why was I feeling that way though? It would be wonderful to have a father again. Wouldn't it?

Mom took the news rather quietly. I saw her exchange a quick look with Mr. Donelly. She seemed to be watching me carefully.

"That's great, Cath. I'm sure you'll love having your father close by."

I had a feeling that she wanted to say more, but I wasn't ready to hear it yet. I had a feeling that I would have more to say, too, once I had time to absorb the news. Without knowing exactly why I did it, I went over to my mother and hugged her. I'm not usually very physically affectionate with her. Don't get me wrong, I love my mother, and she knows that, but I just sort of outgrew the touching stage with her.

"Can we talk about this tomorrow?" I asked. Mom seemed relieved.

I went back to my room. I had a sudden urge to take the phone off the hook. I had enough to think about for one night.

Chapter Four

I woke up the next morning cursing Bulldozer Boy. I was almost as stiff and sore as I was after the first time I did the Jane Fonda Workout. I was glad it was Friday so that I would have a weekend to recuperate. Actually, once I stood for fifteen minutes in a warm shower, I felt much better. Unfortunately, that put me behind schedule getting ready for school, and I had to rush around madly to leave by 7:10. Also, there was a note for me on the refrigerator door.

Cath—

> *Please get the following at the store:*
> *1 lb. hamburger, extra lean*
> *1 box macaroni*
> *3 or 4 tomatoes*
> *Parmesan cheese*
> *1 head lettuce*
> *2 green peppers*
> *some fresh mushrooms*
> *3 hard rolls*

> *Don't bother starting dinner—it's John's turn.*
> *Hope you have a better day at school today.*
>> *Love you,*
> > *Mom*

I had to laugh. After last night's meal, I'm sure Mr. Donelly enthusiastically volunteered to cook tonight. I shoved the list in my pocketbook and dashed out to the trusty red VW bug that is, for all practical purposes, mine. As long as I run Mom's errands for her, I get to drive to school. She used to take the bus to work; now she and Mr. Donelly drive in together in his car. It's fine with me. I hate school buses, and I'd rather go to the grocery store than ride a bus twice a day.

The first six periods went fine, but after yesterday, I didn't get lulled into a false sense of security. Mary is in my third-period English class and we eat lunch together, so I had plenty of time to hear about the glories of Mark.

Finally it was time to walk to seventh-period Spanish class. I seriously considered taking a different route, but I decided against it. First of all, it would be out of my way, but more importantly, I saw this as a test of character. Despite the embarrassment of yesterday, I was going to walk by the Junior Wall—and Tony— calmly and coolly if it killed me. I wasn't going to be run out by Bulldozer Boy.

I rounded the corner, looking carefully ahead, ready to take evasive action if necessary. This time I had stopped first at my locker and gotten rid of everything except my notebook and my Spanish book. If I got rammed again, at least I wouldn't have as much to lose.

What I saw at the Junior Wall, however, completely amazed me. There, stretched across the hall, standing shoulder to shoulder, were Tony, Mark, and six or so other guys. There was a break in the middle wide enough for people to get through, but still there was a small traffic jam. The guys didn't seem to mind all the strange looks they were getting. I walked up to Mark, who was at the center, carefully watching the people going through.

20

"Mark, what are you doing?" I had considered just sneaking through with the rest of the people, but my curiosity got the better of me.

"Hi, Cath. We're waiting for Bulldozer Boy." Mark said this calmly, as if it was completely normal to practically block hallways.

"But why can't you just stand against the wall and watch for him?" After all, he really wasn't that hard to recognize.

"We tried that earlier, but he got away." Mark didn't look too pleased with this particular piece of information.

"What do you mean he got away?" I asked. Suddenly Bulldozer Boy was starting to sound like an escaped convict.

"Well, we saw him barging down the hallway and we yelled at him to stop, that we wanted to talk to him, but he was gone before we could grab him. This time we're not taking any chances."

I can't say I blamed Bulldozer Boy. From what I'd seen of him, he didn't seem like he'd enjoy standing and chatting with eight or so guys. He didn't seem like he wanted to chat with anyone, including Mr. Anderson.

More people merged through the gap in the center of the line. The traffic was starting to clear, and I was about ready to leave for Spanish when Bulldozer Boy rounded the corner behind me. Except for Mark, who had turned to talk to me, the other guys were facing the opposite direction since that's the way Bulldozer Boy had come the previous day. Mark let out a yelp, and the other guys turned just as Bulldozer Boy got to them. Mark had rather unceremoniously shoved me toward the wall. I knew he was trying to protect me, but I sure was getting bashed around a lot lately.

Mark and Tony both moved toward the center of the hallway and extended their arms sideways. Bulldozer Boy was headed straight for them, head down, arms clenched around a big stack of books, bulky brown jacket swirling behind him. He wasn't exactly running, but he was walking faster than I'd ever seen anyone walk, feet thumping loudly.

"Hey, you! Stop right here." Mark's yell had no effect. Bulldozer Boy never slowed a fraction of a step, racing toward the line as if it didn't exist. Seeing him in the center of the hallway, the boys on the right started to move that way. Bulldozer Boy was on a collision course with Mark, Tony, and two others. It was like watching kids on bikes or fools in cars play chicken. The two sides were at each other head on, and it didn't look like either was going to back down.

Two steps before collision, Bulldozer Boy made his move. Without losing speed, he barrelled to the right, racing through the hole between the wall and the end person. I had no idea how he changed direction that fast, but he did. I was right there watching it all, and I still couldn't believe it. The Junior Wall guys were not, to put it mildly, pleased.

I wasn't sure what to say to them and I knew the bell was about to ring, so I walked away and went to Spanish. Sure enough, by the time I got there, Bulldozer Boy was already in his seat. Well, I'm not sure that's exactly accurate. He was in the same seat that he'd been in yesterday, the one in the corner of the back row. He definitely wasn't in the seat assigned to him by Mr. Anderson.

The class waited expectantly while Mr. Anderson took roll. Sure enough, after all the dutiful "heres" there was a silence after the name Robert Sullivan. Mr. Anderson looked up, first toward the assigned seat, then to the back corner. With a slight shake of his head, he finished roll and began class. I guess his heart just wasn't into another round.

Near as I could tell, Bulldozer Boy was winning.

22

Chapter Five

After school, the day just got more and more weird. First of all, I went to the grocery store for my mother. I got everything on the list, which didn't take very long since I know where everything is in the nearest Acme. In fact, I can look at a list and get all the items on it by going through the store from left to right one time. I turned it into a game, making sure that I never had to backtrack an aisle to get something I'd forgotten. I was really good at it. My mother was amazed on one of the rare occasions when she went shopping with me.

Anyway, there I was at the checkout counter with my macaroni and my tomatoes and other assorted ingredients, sneaking looks at the cover of the *National Stargazer* or whatever those strange magazines are that are always in grocery stores. In principle, I am against them, especially since I know that most of the stories are sensationalized lies. I wouldn't pick one up to look inside, and I sure wouldn't buy one. I have to confess, though, that I can't keep from looking at the covers. It's always something like "Woman in Idaho Gives Birth to Three-Headed Albino" or "Is Robert Redford Having a Secret Affair with an Alien from Outer Space?" or "Live to Be 150 By Eating Bee Pollen."

As I was wondering exactly how one gets pollen from bees, I heard a voice in front of me.

"Cath, are you okay?" It was the boy bagging my

groceries at the end of the counter. At first I couldn't figure out who he was and how he knew my name, but then I recognized him as one of the Junior Wall guys. I didn't know his name, and I was surprised that he knew mine. Besides, what did he mean was I okay? On what level was he asking the question?

"Oh hi. Sure, I'm fine," I said, undoubtedly looking a little puzzled.

"Good. Bulldozer Boy really leveled you."

Great. I was famous. Cath Berry, girl most likely to be seen on the floor. Would I ever live that down?

"Just a few bruises. I'm fine, really." Desperately I tried to think of a way to change the subject.

"I just want you to know that we're going to deal with him."

I wasn't sure that I liked the tone of his voice. I knew he thought he was being nice to me, but it sure didn't sound too good for Bulldozer Boy. But why should I worry about that, I told myself angrily. Maybe after the guys had a talk with him, he'd slow down and spare others my humiliation. I pretty much convinced myself that this was all a good deed. Besides, I guess I did like the attention just a little bit.

The boy (I wished I knew his name) finished bagging my groceries and lifted them into the cart.

"Thanks," I said politely. "I'll see you in school on Monday."

"I'll be looking for you," he said, and he smiled.

I walked out of the store in a state of shock. These were the kinds of things that happened to Mary, not to me. Then my normal, old, rational self took over. He didn't mean a thing, I lectured myself. I'm just an excuse for him and his buddies to play big shots. Still, he had said he'd be looking for me. I spent the drive home trying to decide what to wear on Monday. Maybe I'd better buy something new.

The weirdness continued as the evening went on. Mr. Donelly cooked dinner, which wasn't weird but rather was a distinct improvement over my vegetable pie. It was the phone that got things started again. Mom answered it and summoned me.

"I think it's Tony," she said, and she didn't look very pleased about it.

I picked up the receiver in a state of shock.

"Hello?" Probably my mother was wrong. But who could it be?

"Hello, Catherine." No, it was definitely Tony. Not only did I know the voice, but he's the only one who always calls me Catherine rather than Cath.

"Tony!" There. Now what did I say?

"I just wanted you to know that we've got a plan for Monday to take care of Bulldozer Boy. He won't get away from us again."

I almost laughed. I should have said right there and then, "Drop it, Tony. I'm fine. Don't torment the poor kid." But did I? Oh no. Instead I was flattered by all the attention. I didn't stop to think what the consequences might be.

"Thanks for being so concerned." I meant it. After all, this was his second phone call in two days.

"Well, I just don't like the idea of someone hurting you."

That stopped me dead in my thoughts. No one had hurt me worse than Tony, and now he was concerned about someone who knocked me down?

"Tony, I'm fine. Really." What was behind this? Why didn't I ask? How could I ask? What were the right words?

"Catherine, I'm sorry things turned out the way they did with us."

I couldn't believe that I heard right. I had fantasized so many times about hearing something like that.

"I know I don't have the right to ask you to understand. I just want you to know that you were the best thing that ever happened to me."

This couldn't be happening. Tony couldn't be saying these amazing things. I pinched my leg. I seemed to be awake.

"I'll see you in school on Monday. Goodbye, Catherine."

I'm sure I held the receiver for two minutes, just staring at it as if it would explain all of this to me. Finally I put it down and walked back through the living room.

"Was that Tony?" my mother asked.

"Yes," I answered. My voice sounded as if it were coming from far away.

"What did he want, Cath?"

"Just to make sure that Bulldozer Boy didn't do any permanent damage." I was starting to surface again.

Mom looked at me carefully. "Cath, you're not starting all of that again, are you?"

I knew exactly what she meant. After all, she had seen how devastated I was after all the problems Tony had caused. In fact, part of why I broke up with him was so that I could be honest with her again.

"No, Mom," I said.

I guess she believed me. I guess I believed me.

Mom followed me into my room and sat down on the bed. I thought I was in for more questions about Tony, and I wasn't ready for them. I hadn't had time to think all of it through. First the boy at the grocery store and then Tony—plus Mark's concern at school. What a weird day. Nice, but weird.

Luckily for me, my mother had a different topic on her mind—namely, my father.

"Cath, I've had some time to think about last night's news, and I want to talk to you about it."

26

"Sure," I said, relieved. This topic was complicated, too, but it didn't seem as complicated as Tony.

"In some ways it has been hard for me to have your father so far away for so many years," Mom continued. "There have been many times when I haven't been sure I was doing the right thing, when I've wanted the advice of someone else who loves you."

"You've done fine," I said. Really, she had.

"Thanks," she said. "I truly have done the best I'm capable of. I know there were times when I didn't spend enough time with you, times when I was so bombarded with law school or cases at the office that I ignored you unfairly."

"It's okay," I told her. "I've gotten used to it." That didn't come out exactly the way I intended, but she knew what I meant.

"I also know that there are things you've missed by not having a father around, things I couldn't make up for."

"That's not your fault. He was the one who chose to go overseas." She was right. There were times when I had cried for a father, someone to make me feel protected and cherished, but Mom couldn't blame herself for that. Besides, I did know how hard she had tried.

"To be completely honest, though, Cath, there have also been advantages for me in having him so far away."

That took me a little by surprise, but once I thought about it, it made sense. "You mean it would have hurt to have to see him all the time?" I sure understood that from Tony. Tony—no, I couldn't think about him yet.

"Yes, it would have hurt for a while. But it also was easier for me to have you all to myself. I didn't feel like I had to compete for your love. I didn't have to

27

risk that you would decide you wanted to live with him rather than with me."

I looked at my mother in amazement. "Mom, how could you worry about such a thing? Of course I'd live with you. I can't imagine anything else. You're the one who's been with me for the last four years."

"Yes, Cath, but you really haven't had a choice. Your father has been so far away that it wouldn't have been realistic for you to go to him. Now, though, he's going to be right here, at least for a while." She shook her head. "I'm sorry. I want you to be happy that you'll be able to see your father. He's a good man, and you'll enjoy him. Plus, I want him to see how terrific his daughter has turned out. I guess I'm just feeling a little insecure."

"Mom, you don't have a thing to worry about. You couldn't get rid of me if you wanted to."

She gave me a hug and headed for the door. She still looked a little worried.

"Mom, have you talked to Mr. Donelly about this? Maybe he'd love to have you all to himself."

She whirled around and glared at me. "Cath, that's not funny. Don't you even dare . . ."

"Just a joke, Mom, just a joke." The glare faded and we both laughed a little.

See, I said it was a weird day. Two, count them, *two* boys were going to be looking for me in school on Monday. One of them was Tony. My *mother* was admitting to being insecure. All that was left was for Mr. Donelly to get weird on me. With that there was a knock on my bedroom door.

"Cath? May I speak to you for a moment?" It was Mr. Donelly. I couldn't stand it. I had to laugh. I'm sure he was a little put off by my response.

"Sure. Come on in." Why not? I might as well see what he could add to the confusion.

"Cath, you know that I have never tried to become a father figure to you."

"No, you haven't." Mr. Donelly was a smart man. He knew better than to try the impossible. Besides, he seemed rather remote and formal to me a lot of the time. I could tell how much he liked my mother, but he hadn't become someone I confided in, someone I could be completely open with. I truly enjoyed tormenting him and I liked him, but a father figure? No way.

"I just want you to know that I have enjoyed getting to know you these past six months. You are not a typical teenager. I see a lot of your mother in you."

I wasn't sure what he meant by that "typical teenager" comment, but I decided to cut him a break and consider it a compliment. "Thank you," I said. I still wasn't sure what the point of this conversation was.

"I just wanted to tell you that." He left the room, looking rather confused. I don't know what he had intended to accomplish, and I'm not sure that he did either.

I sat in silence for a few minutes, hardly daring to breathe. I finally relaxed when nothing else happened. That was fine with me. I had enough to think about.

Chapter Six

They caught Bulldozer Boy on Monday. I was there at the time, and I did nothing to stop it. How could I have been so totally stupid? I just didn't know where it would lead. That's no excuse, but it's the truth.

Of course, the confrontation took place at the Junior Wall before seventh period. Until that point, Bulldozer Boy had not crossed paths with Tony, Mark, and David. According to Mary, my constant source of information, David was the boy who worked at the Acme. She was most pleased that he would be looking for me. She also said she'd find out more about him. That had me worried. Mary knows just about everything simply because she's Mary. Mary actually working on finding out about someone would be amazing.

I was walking to Spanish, and I have to admit that I had been anticipating it all day. After all, the only three boys in the school who acted like I was alive would all be at the Wall, and all of them, in their own way, were watching out for me. I figured I'd better get there and give them someone to watch out for. I had just said hello when all the excitement began.

First of all, Tony, Mark, David, and the rest of the crew were once again blocking the hallway. This time, though, they were scouting in both directions, and Bulldozer Boy had no chance of surprising them. We almost felt him coming before we could see him. The hall was crowded with kids, but we could see the masses sort of divide in the middle. We could also hear assorted complaints being yelled as people bumped into other people, an unavoidable result of clearing that path. Then, a few seconds later, we could see Bulldozer Boy. He looked just the same as he had before, hair sticking out, the same dark brown jacket. Tony, Mark, and David moved into a V formation in the center of the hallway, and the other guys blocked off the sides. I scrunched up against the wall.

Bulldozer Boy had the advantage of momentum, and I could see his head moving rapidly from side to side, but there was no escape. What he did next amazed me, although I guess after my collision with him I shouldn't have been surprised. Bulldozer Boy simply lowered his head and, without slowing down even a little bit, plowed right into the center V. For a moment, I thought he was through. Mark was knocked off balance into Tony, who almost sent David reeling. The three regained their balance, however, and grabbed Bulldozer Boy by the shoulders, shoving him unceremoniously into the wall right next to me. I could hear Bulldozer Boy's labored breathing, see those strange aqua eyes as they darted frantically around, looking for an escape. Tony, Mark, and David were right on top of him, however, and the other guys made a larger ring around them. I stayed where I was, a silent, frozen spectator.

Bulldozer Boy lowered his head and took a step, which was definitely a mistake. The guys did not take kindly to any kind of movement on his part, not after they had put so much effort into capturing him. Mark and Tony both shoved him, hard, and I heard Bulldozer Boy's head hit against the cement block wall. Bulldozer Boy struggled momentarily to get away from them, but the circle moved closer and he had nowhere to go.

"We want to have a little talk with you," said Mark.

Bulldozer Boy's head was down, his body hunched over. He made absolutely no response.

"We don't like the way you run people down in the hallways," Mark continued. The ring of guys voiced their agreement.

Tony was the next to speak. "Yeah, you ran down a good friend of ours last week, and she could have been seriously hurt."

I had an absurd urge to display the bruise on the back of my elbow that had turned from purple to an ugly, mustard-yellow color. Somehow, though, I didn't think I'd better say anything. I stayed where I was, hidden by the guys yet able to peek through at Bulldozer Boy by leaning my head against the wall.

"If you ever touch her again, you're going to have to answer to us." That was David. I couldn't believe it. It sounded like a line out of some old-time Western movie. The problem was, I loved it. I really loved it. I had spent the first part of high school being invisible—until Tony started dating me, at least—and here I had three guys championing my safety. I felt like a princess surrounded by knights in shining armor. Well, that might be exaggerating just a trifle. After all, I'm not exactly princess material, and my knights were in jeans and Docksiders. Still, I felt important, valued. I felt like applauding.

While all of this was going on, more and more students had gathered. They couldn't see what was happening, but that didn't matter. Suddenly, from the edge of the crowd, someone called out "Teachers coming," and the audience quickly melted away. Tony and Mark started to move back but then suddenly closed in on Bulldozer Boy again. Again they shoved him; again I heard his head hit the wall.

"We'll be watching for you," Tony said quietly. Then they stepped back.

The second there was clear space, Bulldozer Boy shot off. He was off down the hall, gathering speed with every step. The guys watched him in amazement. He bounced off an unsuspecting student leaning over a water fountain and was gone.

The guys looked at me, and I looked at them. "Thanks," I said. "I appreciate your help." Then I left for class.

I had to rush to get to Spanish, but even at my fastest I moved slowly compared to Bulldozer Boy. I found myself experimenting. How was it possible to walk that fast? He definitely did walk, not run, but at an amazing speed. I tried to duplicate it, but then suddenly realized how strange I must look. Luckily, when I looked around, the halls were empty. I had to remember my resolution for the year—cool, calm Cath. Sure. I dashed into Spanish with the bell.

As soon as I got inside the door, I have to admit that my eyes went straight to that back corner. Sure enough, there was Bulldozer Boy. The only difference was, when I looked at him, he looked right back at me. I had never seen him make eye contact with anyone, including Mr. Anderson, and it took me by surprise. I looked away, feeling somehow guilty. Had he seen me in the hallway, or had the circle of guys completely hidden me? I sat down in my seat, and for a few minutes I pretended I was finding the right page in my book. I couldn't stand it, though. I had to look back. I faked a cough, pretending to turn my head to the side out of politeness. Of course, I turned so that I could look back in the corner. Bulldozer Boy's eyes were riveted on mine. As I glanced, his hand went up and touched the back of his head.

I wheeled back around, my face hot. Why did I feel

so uneasy? After all, I was the one who had been knocked to the floor. I reached over and rubbed my bruised elbow.

There. Did that make us even?

Chapter Seven

As near as I could tell, life around school got rougher and rougher for Bulldozer Boy. He was definitely singled out as this year's scapegoat. And he soon became the talk of the school. I'm not sure if word about the incident at the Junior Wall spread, or if Bulldozer Boy's behavior was enough to make him famous without any help. It seemed like everywhere I turned, people were talking about the strange new kid who plowed through the halls and always wore the same brown jacket and never combed his hair. Nobody seemed to know any more about him, except for those who knew that some junior guys had beaten him to a pulp. That, of course, was what rumors turned the Junior Wall incident into. Gossip had it that Tony, Mark, David, and fifteen others had punched Bulldozer Boy in the face, bloodied his nose, dropped him to the floor, and kicked him in the ribs. The kids spreading the story, of course, claimed to have seen it all.

Through it all, there was one common element, and that was the name Bulldozer Boy. I never heard one person refer to him as anything else. I knew from Spanish class that his name was Robert Sullivan, but I never once heard anyone use it except for Mr. Anderson when he called roll. All over school, it was Bulldozer Boy.

The "talk" with the guys didn't slow Bulldozer Boy

down one bit. From what I saw of him, he might even have picked up a little more speed. After all, he was probably getting in shape now that he'd been doing his race walking for a while. From what I heard, he had bumped into lots and lots of people, but the collisions didn't seem to be as bad as mine. At least these victims stayed on their feet, which allowed them to retain a little dignity, unlike me with my sprawl. I guess what happened was that word had spread so thoroughly that everyone was at least a little on the lookout for him. I sure know I always kept looking around, and I moved cautiously around corners. Besides, now he almost had an early warning system. Whenever kids heard or saw him coming, they would begin saying "Bulldozer Boy, Bulldozer Boy," over and over, with the people in front picking up the chant. The motivation behind it was mean. It was a mocking chorus, not a cheer, but whatever the reason, it warned us all to clear a path.

There were some, of course, who did more than chant. I heard the stories, not because people confided in me, but because it was a noisy topic of conversation in classes before the bell rang. Time and time again, kids stuck their feet out into his path, deliberately trying to trip him. He seemed to have an uncanny sense of balance, though; no matter how fast he was moving, he never fell and he never slowed down. Then they resorted to larger obstacles. They threw gym bags into his path, even the trash can out of one of the class-rooms. Always, though, maybe because his head was low, his eyes looking down anyway, Bulldozer Boy stepped on or over the obstacles, frantic to keep on his way.

One day someone threw a firecracker in the boys' bathroom and Bulldozer Boy nearly tore the door off its hinges barging out. Someone told me the look on Bulldozer Boy's face was one of sheer panic.

Then, of course, there were the verbal taunts. Beyond the Bulldozer Boy chant there were others, far worse than that. I guess he made the perfect target. No matter what anybody said, he never responded, never fought back. Even the most cowardly could act big and tough without any danger of getting his face punched in. There sure were some who found that irresistible. Some days when I saw Bulldozer Boy racing for Spanish class, there was a trail of kids following him, imitating him, laughing at him, yelling at him. He just kept right on going.

And the Junior Wall guys weren't the worst. They yelled out to him sometimes, laughed sometimes, but they didn't blockade the hall anymore. As long as they didn't get knocked down, and as long as they weren't sticking up for someone they knew, they were content to let Bulldozer Boy be a daily joke. In fact, I think they would have missed his daily appearance before seventh period.

As the days went on, it became easier to talk to Tony and Mark and David. I only stopped at the wall for a minute or two, just long enough for greetings and a few comments about the day. To be honest, I still had a lot of trouble meeting Tony's eyes, but I could now be in his presence for several minutes without feeling like a fool. I thought that was progress. In a way, it made me angry. I could look at Mark or David or any of the other guys and it was fine. Sure, they made me a little nervous. After all, they were guys, and I was Cath, the one Mary called a social reptile. It was different looking at Tony, however. He still got to my heart and my stomach. Maybe it was because he had kissed me, held me, told me he loved me. After all, he was still the only guy who had ever done that. Maybe it was because even though I was the one who had broken up with him, and even though I still believed that I had done the right thing, part of me wanted to believe that he had changed. Maybe he didn't drink anymore, or hate his parents, or have a negative outlook on everything in the world. Maybe he didn't cut school or refuse to accept responsibility for his actions anymore. Maybe I had given up on him too soon.

These kinds of thoughts tormented me every time I saw Tony. I wanted to talk to him, ask him, but I couldn't. The Junior Wall wasn't the place for serious conversation, and Tony hadn't called me again. I didn't want to call him. Besides, I was afraid. I was afraid that I *would* fall back under Tony's spell, which would make my mother and Mary angry since they'd seen the damage he'd done the first time around. Besides, what if I trusted Tony again and he really hadn't changed? I just didn't want to risk that.

Then, of course, there was the fact that I *had* broken up with Tony. I sure hadn't heard of many guys who gave a girl a second chance after that. Why risk rejection again? Other than the phone calls, Tony certainly hadn't pursued me. Those phone calls, I convinced myself, were just concern that he would have for any friend who might be hurt. But what about that comment that I was the best thing that had ever happened to him? Words come cheap, I convinced myself. Maybe he was drunk, or just nostalgic. I didn't want Tony back, and he didn't want me. I just had to convince my heart and stomach of that.

Meanwhile, it was nice to be on speaking terms with the Junior Wall guys. I knew Mark was on the soccer team, so I could always ask him about that, and I could tease David about what the hot news was from the grocery store checkout lanes. Actually, he had some funny stories to tell from there. My favorite one was about a man, about forty or so, who was standing in line behind an attractive woman. David saw him reach up and pinch the woman's butt. She wheeled around and told him firmly but politely to keep his hands to himself. He pleaded innocent, saying he was minding his own groceries. She turned back around. Not a minute later, he reached up and pinched her again. This time, according to David, the woman turned around, picked up the nearest object, which happened to be a large can of cling peaches, and slugged the guy over the head with it. Then she yelled, full volume, "I told you to keep your hands to yourself. The next time you feel like pinching some woman, you just remember what happened this time. Do you understand?" Of course, all of the customers, cashiers, and David were glued to the action. From a couple of lanes over, someone applauded. The man was holding his head, his face red. He opened his mouth like he was considering arguing. The woman picked up a jar of spaghetti sauce, and the man seemed to reconsider. The woman calmly waited while her groceries were totaled, paid her bill, and waited for David to bag them. As she got ready to leave, she took the can of peaches out of one of the bags and rolled it back to the man. David said he laughed now every time he saw a can of peaches.

It was fun hearing stories like that. Sometimes I felt like my life was boring in comparison. I could feel my life settling into a routine again—school, errands if I'd been left a note on the refrigerator door, dinner, homework, talk to Mary or watch television or read, go to bed, start again the next day. It wasn't bad, just a little predictable. How was I to know that one day predictable would look wonderful and safe?

Chapter Eight

Before I knew it, my father was home. I had gotten the letter with all the information about his flight, and I drove to the airport on a cool evening in late September to pick him up. The whole way to the airport, I felt weird. Part of me was all excited. After all, I hadn't seen my father in two years, and it would be great to see him. Part of me was a little scared, though. After all, I had only seen my father twice in four years, and each of those times had been a whirl-wind few days when he had to come back to town on business. Sure, my father had known and loved the little girl that I was when he and my mother divorced, but what about the person I was now? What if he didn't like the way I looked or acted or talked? Besides, a little voice whispered in the back of my brain, if he really loved me, would he have only seen me twice in four years? Couldn't he have stayed closer to home than Saudi Arabia, or at least couldn't he have found a way to see me more often? Look at all the things he didn't know about. Yes, I wrote him letters, but I had to admit they were on the boring side. They were mainly about school and things like that. He didn't know about Tony, or about how Mary and I had changed in the last few years. He didn't know *me* anymore.

The other part of me battled all of these negative

thoughts. He'll like you, it said. He sort of had to—after all, I was his only daughter, his only child. Besides, it would be exciting getting to know him all over again. It would be like getting back in touch with an old friend—except he wasn't an old friend, he was my *father*, for heaven's sake.

All of this fussing got me to the airport and to the waiting area where his flight was due to arrive. I was nervous, checking the television monitor fourteen times to make sure that I was at the right concourse, checking his letter to make sure that I had the right airline, the right flight number. Of course his flight was late, and by the time it arrived, I was pacing around like a caged leopard, sure that his plane had crashed or been hijacked to Libya.

Finally the plane landed, and I waited for the passengers to clear customs. Just when I was sure that my father had missed the flight, I saw him walking toward me. He looked older, and tired, and I suddenly was afraid he wouldn't even recognize me. I didn't exactly want to go up and introduce myself, so I waited until he was about ten feet away and then ran up to him. I threw my arms around as much of him as I could, considering he was carrying two briefcases, and said, "Hi, Dad. I was afraid you'd missed your flight."

There, I thought. That ought to give him a clue. To give him credit, he did seem to recognize me.

"Cath! How's my girl?" He hugged me back, and the briefcases banged me in the back. It was enthusiastic, if not particularly comfortable. Then I noticed him looking around. "Where's your mother?" he asked.

That took me by surprise for a moment. Wasn't it enough that I was there? "She's at home," I said, somewhat shortly. After all, they *were* divorced. What did he expect, kisses and roses?

"How is she, Cath?"

How was she? What about me? "She's good," I replied. "She's busy and happy." Without you, I mentally added, and with Mr. Donelly. What had happened? My father had been home for about forty-five seconds and already I was angry with him. This would never do.

"I can't believe she let you drive to the airport alone after dark," Dad continued.

"It wasn't dark when I got here," I answered, as if that somehow made a big difference. "She lets me drive wherever I want. I've been here before. I know the way."

"I just don't think it's safe for a young girl to be out alone," Dad said. He had begun walking, and I tagged along, feeling like I was about five years old. There had been many times when I had missed being Daddy's little girl, but this wasn't exactly what I had in mind.

"Where are you staying?" I asked in order to change the topic before I got even more annoyed.

"I'll stay in a hotel for a week or so," Dad replied. "The company is shipping home my belongings, and in the meantime I'll have some time to find an apartment." He didn't look too pleased with any of this. I wondered if the apartment Mr. Donelly was supposed to live in was still available. I was going to mention it when it dawned on me that I had never mentioned to Dad that Mr. Donelly was living with Mom and me. Somehow I had felt awkward about it, as if it wasn't my news to tell. I wondered if Mom had told him. This was getting complicated. Suddenly all I wanted was to go home.

Of course it took about an hour for the luggage to

be unloaded, and by the time Dad's arrived, I had watched the carousel go around until I was dizzy.

Finally we could leave, and I welcomed the cool air after the stifling atmosphere of the airport. We walked through the parking garage in silence, finally reaching the red VW. I took out the keys and unlocked the passenger side door, helping Dad shove his suitcases into the cramped back seat. Then I started walking toward the driver's side.

"I'll drive, Cath." It was an order, not a request.

Somehow that didn't sit too well with me. I had driven safely to the airport to meet his plane, and I certainly could drive safely home. "That's okay, Dad," I said. "I know exactly how to get us out of here and into town."

"I said I'll drive." With that he took the keys out of my hand, unlocked the door, and got in. Immediately he moved back the seat and adjusted the mirror. What was he doing to what I considered *my* car? I was fuming as I got in the passenger's side.

"Fasten your seatbelt, Cath." He didn't even give me a chance to do it on my own before he told me to. I always fasten my seatbelt. I just hadn't gotten to it yet. Next he'd be telling me to finish eating my peas and to brush my teeth.

"Yes, Daddy," I said sweetly. My mother would have picked up the sarcasm in a second. Dad didn't seem to notice. I sat in silence as he left the parking garage, and I didn't say a word as he got in the wrong lane. I only yelped softly when he had to cut across two lanes of traffic to get on the I-95 ramp, and I only made a minor production of tightening my seatbelt and double-checking that the latch was secure. My mother would have been proud of me—maybe.

I listened quietly while Dad talked about the shifting policies in the engineering firm he worked for, and how all of the non-critical personnel were being pulled out of the Middle East and based back in the United States. I wanted to ask him how it felt to be non-critical, but I didn't. I was upset at how upset I was. I mean, here I was with my father for the first time in years, and I was angry and having to fight a tremendous urge to be nasty. This wasn't the way it was supposed to be. I decided that silence was the best I could do, and Dad didn't seem to notice.

Finally we arrived at the Hilton that is on the outskirts of Wilmington. Dad said that the company had already taken care of booking him a suite, and sure enough, the desk clerk had his room key waiting for him. I rode up in the elevator with Dad and the bellhop, then waited for the door to be opened, the suitcases deposited.

Dad looked around and shrugged his shoulders. "Well, it's nice enough but it sure isn't home." What home did he mean—whatever kind of home he'd had for the past four years in Saudi Arabia, or the home we'd had before the divorce? I was too tired to try to figure it out.

"I'd better go. I have school tomorrow." Good old school, always the perfect excuse.

"I have to check in with the office, but I'll call you sometime in the late afternoon or early evening," Dad said.

"Fine," I answered. "I'll talk to you then." With that I left, and I had to admit that mainly what I felt was relief. I almost crashed the VW leaving the parking lot. I forgot that the seat was pushed back, and I couldn't fully reach the clutch or the brake. Once that was solved, I drove home in a daze, trying to figure out exactly what had gone wrong in what I had hoped would be the perfect father-daughter reunion.

Chapter Nine

After I got home that night, I had a long talk with my mother. I hadn't meant to complain about my father, but I couldn't help it. I told her everything, figuring that she would understand. I know I'm lucky to have a mother who I can talk to, but that communication is something we both have worked on. Sometimes I've told her things I never thought she would forgive, and every time she has forgiven. It might take her a few days, but she always does it. What's even better is that once something is resolved with Mom, she never throws it back up in my face. I'm afraid that I haven't inherited that generosity, but I work on it.

Anyway, I told her how annoyed Dad had made me. She sure seemed to understand. Once I thought about it, I realized that she *had* divorced the man, so she must be aware of some of his faults. I hesitated to discuss one particular issue with her, but I knew it had to come out.

"Mom, have you ever told Dad that Mr. Donelly lives with us?"

"No. Have you?"

We looked at each other with what must have been matching looks, half puzzled, half embarrassed.

"It just never came up in the letters I wrote to Dad, and our phone conversations are always so brief that I

45

didn't want to mention it. Besides, I sort of thought it was your news."

"Cath, I'm not embarrassed to tell your father. After all, we've been divorced for years, and I'm free to live my own life, just as he's been free to live his, and besides, I don't feel that John and I are doing anything wrong by living together, and I don't feel that we're harming you . . ."

"Hold on, Mom, slow down," I said, afraid that she would pass out if she didn't take a breath soon. "Nobody is saying that you're doing anything wrong. Don't be so defensive."

There was a moment of silence before my mother answered. "Am I being defensive?" she asked.

"Sounds like it to me, and I tend to recognize that kind of behavior," I laughed. Mom had once said that I defended myself before I was ever accused of anything. That was how she always knew when I had a guilty conscience.

"Well, your father always has had the ability to make me feel like a flighty adolescent in the face of his sober, rational mind."

"Mom, you're a lawyer now, and you wear suits and have an office and you're allowed to live with anyone you want to."

Mom laughed. "And what a relief that all is," she said, "except for the suits. It's just that for some odd reason, people don't seem to trust a lawyer in jeans and a sweatshirt with Bullwinkle the Moose on it. I've never quite understood why, but I've learned to live with it."

Another good thing about Mom is that when there is a problem, she believes in confronting it immediately. There's none of that dragging things out with her.

"Okay, Cath," she said. "Your father is calling tomorrow. We need a game plan. I know I need to see him, and in some ways I want to see him, so when he calls tomorrow, let's invite him for dinner."

"Great," I said. "He'll probably cut my meat up for me and tuck the napkin under my chin." Mom laughed. I could tell that she knew she shouldn't, but she did anyway.

"Now," Mom continued, "we need to consider John."

"We could hide him in the closet," I suggested.

"Cath, that's not funny," Mom replied, but I saw her eyes twinkle. "Besides, there's not enough room in any of them, and I don't have time to clean before tomorrow."

"You could make him work late at the office," I suggested, knowing that I was pushing my luck.

"Yes, or I could make him hide in the bushes, or visit his aunt in Hoboken, or do any number of other things, but I'm not going to."

"Oh no," I said dramatically, flinging back my head and putting my hand to my brow. "That can only mean that you plan to confess to my father that you're living in sin."

"Well," she said slowly, "maybe Hoboken isn't such a bad place to spend a Friday night. And John really doesn't spend enough time with his relatives." After we both finished laughing, she said more seriously, "Cath, I'm not going to hide John from your father, most of all because that's not fair to John. It would make it look like I'm ashamed of him or something, and I'm not. He's a fine man, and I enjoy his presence in our home."

"Good luck," I said. "I'll be at Mary's if you need me."

"You will not," she laughed. "You'll be right here enjoying every moment of my discomfort."

With that, Mr. Donelly walked in. I left Mom alone to fill him in on the good news.

The next evening went beyond my worst expectations. Dad didn't cut my meat for me, but that would have been better than what he actually did—or at least tried to do.

When he called, I invited him for dinner and he sounded pleased to accept. He had a rented car so he planned to be at our apartment by 7:00. Mom came home early from the office, and we straightened up the living room, cleaned the bathroom, and started dinner. We even fixed some of Dad's favorite foods—marinated London Broil with baked potatoes, fresh cauliflower with cheese sauce, creamed corn, and a big salad. Mr. Donelly was due home about 6:30, and we had everything under control, or so we thought.

Normally Mr. Donelly is a very poised, controlled man. I swear that he must roll out of bed in the morning with every hair in place. He chooses his clothes carefully, he chooses his words carefully, and he makes me want to leap out of corners and muss him up. It's not that I don't like him; it's just that I'm never quite sure exactly where my body parts are, and being around him can make me feel more awkward and out of control than usual.

When he came in that night, though, he looked nervous. As soon as he walked in, I could see him scouting around for my father. It was only after he was sure he wasn't there that he kissed my mother hello.

"Angela," he said to my mother, "are you sure that you don't want some privacy in which to get reacquainted with your husband, your ex-husband, that is?" He said it sincerely, but I could tell that he was afraid that she would say yes.

"Nonsense," my mother replied. "We talked about this last night. I want you to meet William. After all, you are the two most important men in my life.'' With that, she sweetly kissed him. ''Now take off your jacket and help me make this salad.''

Promptly at 7:00 the doorbell rang, and I went to let in my father. He had a brown bag in his hand, and he did not offer it to me. My mother came out of the kitchen, and for a moment they just looked at each other. It was definitely awkward. Then my mother closed the gap and gave my father a big hug. He looked relieved and hugged her back. I stood there and wondered if Mr. Donelly was peeking out of the kitchen watching this touching scene.

''Here, Angela,'' my father said. ''I remembered that this was your favorite wine. It took me three stops to find it.''

My mother took the bag and pulled out the bottle. It must have been expensive, because she told him he shouldn't have. By this point, I was really getting curious about the fourth member of our dinner party, so I went out into the kitchen to look for Mr. Donelly. I found him leaning against the counter, looking absolutely miserable. That made me like him even more.

''Come meet my father,'' I said. After all, what would be gained by delaying this any further?

By the time Mr. Donelly and I made it to the living room, my parents were already there. My father's face registered considerable surprise. He looked from Mr. Donelly to me and back to Mr. Donelly. For a moment I think he thought that Mr. Donelly was my date or something. I almost giggled. Actually, I looked at my mother rather searchingly. If she didn't come over to Mr. Donelly soon, the poor man was going to fall over. Finally she crossed to him and put her hand on his shoulder. He tensed as if he had been hit. Poor Mr. Donelly.

"William, I'd like you to meet John Donelly. He is a colleague of mine at the office, and a dear friend." My mother sounded a little nervous and a little defensive. It was an interesting combination.

My father did not exactly smile warmly, but he did shake Mr. Donelly's hand and murmur the obligatory "Pleased to meet you." I was looking at my mother, and she met my eyes and shook her head slightly. I could almost read her mind. She hadn't wanted to come right out and announce that Mr. Donelly lived with us, but she also knew that "dear friend" didn't exactly do the situation justice. Poor Mom.

We all sat down, and the conversation quickly went to life in Saudi Arabia, which was fine with me. My mother, Mr. Donelly, and I had plenty of questions about the culture, language, food, customs, and people, and my father seemed glad of the opportunity to be the expert. True, he did seem to look at Mr. Donelly a little harshly, but maybe that was my overactive imagination.

Dinner went smoothly, with my father full of compliments for my mother's cooking, and for her consideration in fixing his favorites, and for how attractive she looked, and for how nicely she had fixed up the apartment, and for everything else in sight. Mr. Donelly didn't say a word through that stretch. In fact, he started looking a little tense around the mouth and eyebrows again. Mom was starting to relax, maybe because of the wine, maybe because of the compliments. I, on the other hand, was getting more boggled by the minute. There my father was lavishly praising my mother, the woman he had divorced and not seen in years, and there was my mother seeming to enjoy it in front of her live-in lover, still masquerading as a "dear friend."

Everything was fine until after dinner when we

moved back into the living room. My father excused himself to use the bathroom, which none of us gave any thought to. My mother used the time to move closer on the sofa to Mr. Donelly and to run her hand down his arm and briefly take his hand in hers. He did not act especially thrilled; in fact, he moved down the sofa so that there was once again space between them.

When my father came out of the bathroom, he was a changed man. Normally his blue eyes are rather calm; now, however, they looked more gray than blue, and there were definitely storm warnings in them. His first question came out of nowhere, taking us all by surprise.

"So, John, where do you live?"

I have to give Mr. Donelly credit. He only paused for a few seconds before he said, "I used to live in the Plaza View Apartments, but they were converted into condominiums and I didn't want to purchase my unit. For the past six months I've been living here with Angela and Cath."

"You have been living here in the same apartment as my daughter?" My father suddenly sounded like an attorney himself, and an angry one at that. I was still confused. Why had my father brought this up so suddenly? Then a light bulb went on in my brain. The bathroom. On the shelf beside the sink there were Mr. Donelly's shaving stuff, cologne, deodorant. That's what had tipped off my father. I returned my concentration to the conversation, which my mother had entered.

"Yes, of course with Cath. The three of us have made out just fine." She looked at me, but I was speechless.

"And I must assume that since this is only a two-bedroom apartment, and since this man is your dear friend, this has not been a purely platonic arrangement?'' My father was definitely getting hostile by this time. My mother was no longer smiling, and Mr. Donelly was practically quivering with tension.

"How dare you question how I lead my life?'' my mother said, quietly but with great force. "You lost that right on the day our divorce became final—if you ever really had it.''

"That's where you're wrong, Angela,'' my father said, matching her intensity. "I have the right to question anything that involves my daughter.''

Mr. Donelly entered into it next. "I don't believe that my living here is doing any damage to Cath,'' he said. My father interrupted before he could continue. "That's for me to decide, not you.''

Next it was my turn to get angry. I couldn't stand this. I couldn't sit and listen as if I were invisible. "What about me?'' I asked, and I have to admit that my voice wasn't quite as quiet as theirs. I didn't exactly yell, but it wasn't a whisper either. "Don't I have anything to say about this?''

"No,'' was my father's snapped response. "You're still a child.''

"A child?'' I asked. "I'm almost seventeen years old. I think I would know if I were being damaged or not.''

"Your mother is carrying on an affair in your own home, and I don't consider that an appropriate environment for a child. Now that I am here permanently again, I can see that I will have to resume some control over your well-being.''

My mother catapulted off of the sofa, and stood before my father, who calmly, slowly raised himself out of the chair in which he was sitting. "How dare you?'' she shouted. "How dare you virtually abandon your daughter for four years, *four years*, and then act as if you know what's good for her? You've been back

52

for twenty-four hours, and you're passing judgment on my life and hers?''

''I know what constitutes a moral upbringing, and it doesn't look as if you can provide that.''

I couldn't believe this was happening. After years of fantasizing about what it would be like to have a father around, now I had the answer—at the moment it was a nightmare.

''Mom has done a good job of raising me, and there's nothing immoral about Mr. Donelly,'' I said in a shaky voice. My anger was changing into the edge of tears. It wasn't exactly what I had meant to say, but it would have to do.

''William, I'm sure that if we discuss this calmly and rationally, you will see . . .'' Mr. Donelly seemed the calmest of the lot, but my father was in no mood to listen to him.

''Perhaps a lawyer is whom I should discuss this with,'' he said. With that, he walked to the door and left.

My mother slumped back onto the sofa, and this time it was Mr. Donelly who reached out to her, gently covering her hand with his. I stared at my mother, and she stared back. It seemed almost unbelievable how far downhill the evening had gone.

''Cath, don't worry,'' my mother said in a tired voice. ''There is no legal basis for your father to take you away from me. Besides, you are at an age where your wishes concerning which parent to live with will almost always be the determining factor.''

''But how could he do this? How could he think he could just waltz back into my life and take over like this?''

''I'm as surprised as you are,'' my mother had to admit. ''I've always told you that we had one of the most civilized divorces in history, and that was the truth. Every time we've been in touch over the past four years, he has said that he had total faith in my judgment concerning you. I honestly don't know what brought this on.''

"Perhaps I did,'' said Mr. Donelly.

"How?'' asked Mom.

"It seemed to me that he was taking quite an interest in you tonight,'' Mr. Donelly responded.

"Right,'' Mom said sarcastically. Then, more kindly, she said, "John, William and I were married for years. We share a daughter. But that relationship is over. We both knew it beyond a shadow of a doubt. That's why the divorce was friendly—we both knew that it just wouldn't work any more. It wasn't that I thought he was a terrible person, or that he thought I was a terrible person. It was just that we had grown in different directions, and our lives didn't fit together anymore.''

"Perhaps four years in Saudi Arabia has changed his mind.'' I couldn't decide if Mr. Donelly was being jealous or rational. Maybe he could be both at once. All I knew was that I had had enough.

"I give up. You figure this all out.'' I headed for my bedroom.

"Cath, please don't worry. Everything will be okay.'' My mother looked worried, but her words were somewhat comforting.

"Right,'' I said.

Even I didn't know if I was being serious or sarcastic.

Chapter Ten

We didn't hear anything from my father for the rest of the weekend or for the next week, which, frankly, was fine with me. Mom and Mr. Donelly and I were all a little numb after Friday night's explosion. I have to admit that I was worried. I talked to Mary about it, and she said that my father couldn't possibly convince anyone that my mother was an unfit parent because I was such a model teenager. I laughed at her theory, but she did manage to cheer me up. Still, there was a patchy fog of gloom hanging around the apartment, and it was a relief to go back to school on Monday. At least there was plenty there to occupy my mind.

If my life was not going too well at that point, neither was Bulldozer Boy's. By the end of the day on Monday, he was nowhere in sight, and rumors were swirling. I finally fit together all of the pieces, subtracted half of everything to allow for exaggeration, and came pretty close to the truth, I think. It seemed that Bulldozer Boy was making his normal stampede through the hallway on Monday morning when he ran into Mrs. Brentano. Of course, with Bulldozer Boy that wasn't a "good morning, how are you today" kind of encounter; it was another collision about as spectacular as the one he'd had with me.

To fully understand, though, you have to know about Mrs. Brentano. She was an absolute classic around our school. To begin with, she looked like she was about ninety-seven. I know that school districts have mandatory retirement ages, but it seemed like she had slipped through the system. She was a tiny bird of a woman. Maybe when she was younger she had been about five feet tall, but now she was hunched over and couldn't have stretched beyond four feet six inches. Her silver hair was always in a straggly bun with pieces escaping, and she wore clothes that were so old they were almost fashionable again. She taught French and Latin, and she hadn't only taught older brothers and sisters of her present students, she had taught their parents. Some claimed grandparents, but I think that was going a little too far.

Every year some students gave her a really hard time. Once one of the boys learned how to do a perfect imitation of the secretary in the General Office who calls over the intercom system built into each classroom.

"Mrs. Brentano?" he would say from the back of the room, sounding exactly like the secretary.

Mrs. Brentano would look up at the ceiling. It helped that she always looked at the speaker mounted in the front corner when she answered. "Yes?"

"Would you please send Jimmy Silverman to the General Office?"

"Yes, right away," Mrs. Brentano would answer, and Jimmy would stroll out of class, to the immense delight of his buddies. One day the kid cleared out a third of the class, and then summoned himself to the General Office. Despite all the laughter from the class, Mrs. Brentano never caught on.

Even with the pranks, though, we all sort of looked out for Mrs. Brentano, even those who weren't in her classes. She was such a genuinely sweet lady that eventually almost everyone got tired of taking advantage of her. Actually, she won over some of the real thugs, and they became her guards. I personally saw her come flying out of her classroom one day when there was an argument in the hallway. The two boys weren't fighting yet, but they were up in each other's faces, yelling obscenities. Mrs. Brentano charged right between them, small as she was, and said in her high-pitched voice, "Young gentlemen, I am certain that there is some misunderstanding here, and that you are capable of far better behavior than this. I can see that you are fine young men, and you are in the presence of a lady. I expect you to behave accordingly. Do you understand?"

To the amazement of everyone gathered, the two boys apologized to Mrs. Brentano, saying they wouldn't have used those words if they'd known she was around.

"I know that," she said. "Just remember that I could be your grandmother. Would you want your grandmother to hear such language?"

"No, ma'am," one of the boys answered, and they both walked off rather sheepishly. I have to admit that I was impressed with Mrs. Brentano.

It was unfortunate, then, that Mrs. Brentano became an unintentional victim of Bulldozer Boy. Bulldozer Boy was racing from second- to third-period class, and Mrs. Brentano evidently was coming from the staff center with a big pile of dittos that she had just run off. During the collision, those papers flew like confetti, and Mrs. Brentano ended up in a heap on the floor. She wasn't quite as lucky as I was, though. Because she was so tiny and brittle, an ankle twisted badly in the spill, and she had to be helped down to the nurse's office. One of the assistant principals immediately found Bulldozer Boy and forcibly escorted

57

him to the office; otherwise, a mob would have gone after him.

At first, rumor had it, Bulldozer Boy was going to be recommended for expulsion for assaulting a teacher. What he had done, however, didn't exactly fit the definition of assault, and it certainly hadn't been premeditated. From what I heard, Mrs. Brentano also spoke up in his defense. Supposedly she said that any student in that much of a rush to get to class couldn't be all bad. Ultimately, Bulldozer Boy ended up suspended for three days for "Disruption of the Orderly Process of Education" or some such heading in the Student Code of Conduct. Mrs. Brentano was on crutches for a week and then proclaimed herself fully healed.

I have to admit that those three days had a certain something missing. I still stopped at the Junior Wall on my way to seventh-period Spanish class, but no longer were we all on the lookout. It was relaxing, but I almost missed seeing Bulldozer Boy fly by. Yes, I felt bad for Mrs. Brentano; after all, few knew better than me how painful an encounter with Bulldozer Boy could be. I knew, though, that Bulldozer Boy's head had been down—it always was—and that he hadn't meant to hit her. That didn't make Mrs. Brentano's ankle any less sore, but at least she hadn't been intentionally tripped. Tony and Mark and David, on the other hand, were raring to have another "talk" with Bulldozer Boy. In a way it made me sad. Their reaction to Mrs. Brentano being decked was just like their reaction to my being decked. I had been right after all—their concern was for any victim, not for me.

I have to admit that I also was watching for clues from Tony. I watched for any special eye contact, any words that could have a deeper meaning intended for only me to understand. All I know is that if there were any deeper meanings, they were so deep that even I couldn't pick them up. Tony was friendly, but that was all. I didn't know whether to be relieved or disappointed.

By Friday, Bulldozer Boy had finished serving his suspension and was back in school. I saw him go past, and he hadn't slowed down a footstep. I was amazed—you'd think that after hurting a teacher and being suspended, he would be careful, but that kind of logic didn't seem to apply to Bulldozer Boy. The kids were treating him worse than ever, too.

"Hey, pick on someone your own size," I heard one girl yell at him. "Mrs. Brentano is a bird-woman." I wondered if Mrs. Brentano would have liked *that* defense.

"Why do you always sit out in gym class?" a boy yelled. "Man, anybody can pass gym class. Why won't you come out of the corner?"

"You don't belong here," another girl chimed in. "Get out. Go to some special school for weird people." She had to yell her insults since Bulldozer Boy was already far down the hallway.

I would have remained nothing but an observer if Mr. Anderson hadn't thrown me into closer contact with Bulldozer Boy. On the Friday that Bulldozer Boy returned to school, I was sitting quietly in Spanish class, thinking about my father, waiting for class to begin. I jumped when Mr. Anderson said my name.

"Cath, may I speak to you for a moment, please?" He remained behind his desk, so I had no choice but to go up to him. My mind was in a panic—even though I get good grades, do my homework, and usually pay attention in class, there's something about a teacher asking to speak to you that sends out panic alerts. I frantically searched my brain for wrongdoings, wondering if Mr. Anderson somehow knew that I had penciled English translations in the margin of my Spanish book.

"Cath, I would like to compliment you on the work you've been doing in my class. You've demonstrated an excellent grasp of the language in the short time we've been back in school."

"Thank you." That was a relief, as was the fact that for once he was speaking in English rather than Spanish.

"In light of your performance, I would like to ask a favor of you."

Great, I thought. That "ask" is just for politeness. He can tell me to do just about whatever he wanted. "What is it?" I replied.

"Mr. Sullivan has been absent this week. I would like you to fill him in on the assignments he has missed."

Mr. Sullivan? For a moment the name didn't register. Then it did. Bulldozer Boy.

"Also," continued Mr. Anderson, "we will be starting work on dialogues today which will be written in pairs and then performed in front of the class next week. I would like you to be Mr. Sullivan's partner."

"But he doesn't talk," I blurted out.

"I realize that might be a problem. Do the best you can."

Mr. Anderson opened his roll book and began to take attendance. I walked back to my seat in a daze. How on earth was I supposed to do a dialogue with a partner who had yet to open his mouth? I hated to speak in front of the class under the best of circumstances, and these certainly weren't the best. I stared at Mr. Anderson pleadingly, wanting to refuse his favor, wanting to protest. He must have known because he absolutely refused to meet my eyes.

Sure enough, Mr. Anderson paired up the class for the dialogues. Calmly as could be, he read from his list, "Cath Berry and Robert Sullivan." From all over the room I could hear snickers. I heard somebody say "Now there's a couple—the brain and the Bulldozer Boy." The boy who sat behind me even patted me on the shoulder and said, "Good luck. Better you than me."

Once Mr. Anderson had finished with the list, we were all supposed to pair off with our partner and begin writing. There was a lot of talking and joking and scraping as desks were rearranged. I sat where I was, but I knew that Bulldozer Boy would never come to me. Finally, with a deep sigh, I gathered up my books and looked toward the back corner. Sure enough, there he was, eyes darting around. Resolutely I walked back to him and moved the closest empty desk until it was next to Bulldozer Boy's. He looked at me, then looked away. Once again I noticed those odd aqua eyes.

"Hi," I said, "I'm Cath Berry."

He looked at me, then looked away. Silence.

"You ran into me one day in the hall." There. Maybe that would get a response from him. Silence.

"I'm okay now. I just had some bruises." A little guilt, a little reassurance. Maybe that would get through to him. Silence.

Okay, how about a different topic. "Mr. Anderson wants me to show you what you missed in class this week." Silence.

I decided to plunge ahead. At least then I would have honored Mr. Anderson's request. I opened my Spanish book and showed Bulldozer Boy what passages we had read, what translations we had done for homework, what vocabulary we were responsible for on next week's test. Bulldozer Boy didn't say a word, but at least his eyes were on my book, following what I pointed to. Maybe I was accomplishing something.

Once I had finished telling him what we had covered, I became aware of all the noise surrounding us. Pairs all over the room were leaning together, talking and occasionally laughing, writing hesitantly with plenty of pauses to search through the dictionary in the back of the book. Most of them seemed to be enjoying themselves, and there I was with Bulldozer Boy. I considered matching him silence for silence for the rest of the period, but that didn't seem especially productive. Finally I opened my notebook and turned to a blank sheet of paper.

"We're supposed to write a dialogue where we establish and then solve a problem," I said, as much to myself as to him. Maybe I should write about the problem I was facing right this moment, I thought.

Before I realized what he was doing, Bulldozer Boy grabbed my notebook, pulling it onto his desk and writing on the blank page. When he had finished writing, he shoved it back across to me. I looked at the page in amazement. As nearly as I could translate, he had written in what seemed to be flawless Spanish:

Man: Help! Help! There is a tiger in my yard.

I double checked the dictionary to make sure that it did indeed say tiger. Bulldozer Boy looked at me and then at the paper. Obviously it was my turn. I thought for a moment, then wrote:

Woman: Are you sure that it isn't just a big house cat?

Bulldozer Boy took back the paper and wrote, quickly and with no hesitation:

Man: I've never seen a house cat that is eight feet long and has sharp, pointed fangs that show when he snarls.

Before Bulldozer Boy handed the paper back to me, he penciled in a correction in my sentence.

I first looked at what he had fixed. I hated to admit it, but he was right. I had used the wrong verb ending, and he had substituted the right form. I also had to use the dictionary to translate fangs and snarls, which he had written out without any hesitation. I was impressed.

Back and forth we went, telling the story of the man with the tiger in his yard. Although I looked very carefully, I never found anything I could correct in Bulldozer Boy's sentences. Although I wrote very carefully, he found several more things to correct in mine. Before I realized it, I was having a fine time, making the woman the brave one who solved the problem by convincing the tiger that it really was a friendly kitty who only wanted to lap milk and sleep peacefully in the highest branches of the man's apple tree. It was a silly dialogue, but by the end of the period we had filled several pages, which seemed to be more than many of the others had accomplished.

The only problem came when the bell rang at the end of the period. Moments before, Bulldozer Boy had been peacefully reading over our finished dialogue, but the second the bell rang, he snatched up his books and bolted out of the room, almost having to hurdle my desk in the process. I had to brace myself against the wall to avoid being tipped over.

I watched him in amazement. I couldn't come up with a theory that would even begin to explain him.

Chapter Eleven

When I walked out of Spanish class that day, yet another surprise awaited me. Leaning against the wall right outside the door was Tony. There I was, mind filled with Bulldozer Boy, when suddenly I was confronted by something I had loved to see last year when we were dating—Tony lounging against a wall, waiting for me.

"My motorcycle is broken, and I hate school buses. Could I possibly have a ride home?"

I couldn't believe it. Those were almost the exact same words that he had said last year just when things were starting between us. Then I had been turned into a mute, barely functional zombie by him; this time I didn't feel too much better. That feeling of powerlessness made me angry, though. I was over Tony, wasn't I, and that should mean that I could give him a simple ride home, just like I would any other acquaintance.

"Sure," I said in a voice that only betrayed maybe half of what I was thinking.

"Thanks," Tony said, following me to my locker and then to the parking lot and my car, chatting casually the whole time about his motorcycle and the string of problems he had had with it.

By this time, I was paying only the vaguest attention to Tony's words because inside my head I was chanting, "He's only a boy; it's only a ride," over and over and over again. It didn't help a lot—my palms were sweating, my heart racing—but at least it kept my feet moving and my mouth saying "uh-huh" every now and then.

The familiar feel of the red VW bug surrounding me was, as usual, calming. I was headed in the direction of Tony's house when his words jolted me.

"Catherine, do you have a few minutes to talk? Let's go to the park."

On the surface, that seemed like a simple request, but it wasn't. The park had been our special place, our refuge, the whole time we had dated. Being there with him would bring back too many memories. I had to say no.

"Sure," I said, and made a left turn instead of the right that would lead to Tony's house. Who had said those words? I was amazed. I felt like one of those people in scary movies who was possessed by an alien's spirit.

I really don't remember the rest of the drive to the park. I vaguely remember saying words now and then, and they must have been okay because the conversation seemed to flow along nicely. I parked the car in the familiar lot, and Tony and I walked down to the part of the creek we had always considered ours. We had started dating in the spring, and I had always seen the trees in green. The leaves had started to turn now and, if anything, the setting was even more beautiful with tinges of gold and orange.

We both sat on the flat rock near the creek's edge, and before I knew what was happening, Tony's arm was around me and I was pulled tightly against the familiar but frightening warmth of him. His hand gently touched the side of my face, turning my head toward him. Then, silently, sweetly, he kissed me. One side of me cried out no, don't let this happen; the other side melted. I kissed Tony back.

"I've missed you, Catherine," Tony said, touching my hair, hugging me tight.

"I've missed you, too," a voice said. As if from a distance, I recognized it as mine.

"No one else has made me laugh the way you did," he continued after a moment's silence.

"There's been no one else for me," my voice answered. Even in my highly distracted state, I knew that was a stupid thing to say. Mary had given me lecture after lecture about the fine art of making boys jealous, being slightly remote, implying more than telling, leaving them wanting to know more, and there I was being my brutally honest self.

"I'm glad," Tony said. His second kiss made me think that maybe there were rewards for honesty.

We spent the next half hour kissing, hugging, laughing at nothing, skipping stones—an art Tony had taught me—and talking about nothing that really mattered. I felt wonderful. I felt as if every cell of my body was bursting with energy, coming back to life after a long hibernation. I felt as if I could see better, hear better, smell better than I ever had before. I felt that if I was never happy again, these moments would be enough. If there was a price to pay, it didn't matter.

Eventually, nudged back to reality, we left the park, and I drove Tony home. He kissed me goodbye, and I watched him walk up the driveway of the house he had always claimed to hate because of the father he called the Ogre and the mother who hadn't really wanted a child in the first place. I drove away in a daze, on some kind of automatic pilot that led me home.

I was glad that Mom and Mr. Donelly were still at the office. All I wanted to do was lie on my bed and relive the time I'd just spent with Tony. Unfortunately, that was not to be. In the park, my brain had basically deserted me. I had operated purely on emotion, responding to the pleasure of being held and kissed. I was never cut out to be a romantic heroine, however, because eventually my brain always kicks back in, and this time the rational side of me was not especially pleased.

What the hell just happened, I asked myself. Why did you go through all the pain of breaking up with Tony just to let it start up all over again the first second he wants it to? Where is your self-respect, your determination not to be controlled by someone who basically isn't good for you? Why didn't you say no, you can't have a ride, no we can't go to the park, and take your hands off of me?

Because I hadn't wanted to. That was why. Because Tony still had the ability to make me feel rather than think.

He'll hurt you again, the rational side said. He's changed, the emotional side argued.

Unfortunately, I couldn't get any help with this argument. Normally I would have been on the phone to Mary, or I would have talked to my mother. Neither of those options would do this time, however. I knew that both Mary and my mom would be angry at the idea of my seeing Tony again. They both saw how much he'd hurt me the first time, and somehow I didn't think either of them would be very convinced that he had made dramatic changes.

Today's trip to the park would have to be news I kept all to myself. I didn't especially like that, but on the other hand it almost made the whole thing even more romantic. Just when I was about to turn Tony and me into a modern *Romeo and Juliet*—with a happy ending this time, of course—the phone rang. It's Tony, I thought. He wants to take me out this weekend.

The voice I heard was masculine, but that was all it had in common with Tony's. It was my father.

67

"Cath, I'm at the office, but I'll be free at 5:30. I'll pick you up by 6:00 at the latest."

"Dad, I . . ." That was as far as I got. I didn't have any plans for the evening, but it made me angry that he hadn't even asked. I decided to invent some.

"I'll see you then. I have good news."

The phone went dead while I was still sputtering. I stormed back to my room in a temper, deciding that he could come at 6:00 if he wanted to but that I deliberately wouldn't be home. There. That would show him. I would go to Mary's. No, I couldn't, I remembered. She had a date with Mark. Fine, then I would simply not answer the door, and if Mom and Mr. Donelly were home, they'd have to cover for me.

Eventually though, I calmed down. Dad had had a week to think about how he'd acted the last time I'd seen him, and maybe he was sorry and wanted to make it up to me. Besides, he *had* said that he had good news.

Mom and Mr. Donelly weren't home yet by the time Dad arrived so I left them a note on the refrigerator door and off I went. We filled the silence with talk about school and his job, nothing that really mattered but better than nothing at all. I asked Dad where we were going, and got only a cryptic "You'll see" in return.

Eventually we pulled up in front of an apartment complex about fifteen minutes from home. I followed Dad toward an entranceway, watching as he took out a key and unlocked the door.

"I've rented it completely furnished so everything is all set up," Dad said.

I looked around. Yes, it was a nice apartment with comfortable furniture, curtains, the whole bit. It didn't look especially homey, but it certainly was functional. I followed Dad from room to room.

"It's very nice," I said, wondering if this was the good news. I was glad that Dad had a nice place to live, but that was about it. After he had shown me the master bedroom, he walked to a second bedroom.

"I insisted on a two-bedroom apartment," Dad said. "This bedroom can be yours."

"That's nice," I said, envisioning the occasional night spent staying there, maybe after Dad and I had gone somewhere together.

My father was looking at me rather searchingly. "I fully intend for you to live with me. As you can see, there is plenty of room for the two of us." He put emphasis on *two*.

Then it dawned on me. *That* was supposed to be the good news.

"Dad, I appreciate the offer, but I am very happy with Mom, and I need to stay with her."

"You need to live in a normal, healthy environment."

"Dad, we are very normal and very healthy."

"Now Cath, do you honestly believe that it is normal to live in a household with your mother's lover?"

"Why not? Mom and Mr. Donelly are happy. They care about each other, and they care about me. Mom and I have talked a lot. I know that what she's doing is nothing that I'm ready for yet, but that doesn't mean that it's wrong for her." This whole conversation was starting to seem very strange to me. Why was I defending my mother's living arrangements to my father?

"Well, I believe that I will set a better example for you than your mother is obviously doing."

Now I was really getting angry. "Mom is setting a great example for me. I know that I can talk to her about almost anything, and that's more than I can say for most kids I know and their mothers. And she's honest with me. She asked me before she let Mr. Donelly move in, and she has asked me since if I want him to leave. She's not forcing anything on me. I just

69

like seeing her happy. Besides, Mr. Donelly doesn't take up much space.''

I was doing fine until that last statement, which didn't come out exactly as I had intended it to.

''Cath, I got this apartment with you in mind, and I also have a real estate agent looking for a small house in the vicinity. I intend to provide for you.''

''Well, maybe you should have asked me first. Mom and I have done just fine for the past four years, and we'll continue to be just fine.''

''We'll see about that.''

This was great. I hardly ever argued with anyone, preferring to retreat into silence, to avoid conflict, and there I was practically in a shouting match with my own father. I hated that, but I couldn't back down. I couldn't imagine living anywhere other than with my mother. Did he actually think he could bribe me with a house? He sure didn't know me very well. Then it dawned on me that the absolute truth was he *didn't* know me very well. How could he? There was a huge difference between the twelve-year-old he'd left behind when he went to Saudi Arabia and the person I was now. So much had happened in those years, things that he couldn't understand from letters and quick phone calls. He didn't even know about Tony.

''So how long has your mother known this John Donelly?'' My father interrupted my private thinking.

''I don't know,'' I said honestly.

''What do you mean you don't know?''

''Well, he's been living with us for about six months, but I don't know how long they knew each other before that.''

''And they work in the same office?''

I knew the answer to that one. ''Yes, and sometimes they work together on cases.''

''Just what does your mother see in him?''

Now how was I supposed to answer that one? I mean, I sure had considered Mr. Donelly a little on the boring, conservative side at moments, but Mom seemed happy with him. Maybe he was a phenomenal lover. Maybe he filled up the loneliness. Maybe she loved him for his mind. I didn't know, and why was my father asking? And why was he asking me? And, when it came down to it, what right did he have to ask? Still, I figured I'd better give some kind of answer.

"I guess they have a lot in common." There. That was safe. It also seemed to shut up my father.

My father offered to take me out to dinner, but I said no. I was so tense that I didn't think there was any room for food among the knots in my stomach. We drove home in silence. Just as I was ready to get out of the car, Dad said, "Cath, I really want you to think about the advantages of living with me. Once you get over the initial shock, I'm sure you'll see them."

"I'll think about it," I said, knowing that I wouldn't change my mind but not wanting to start another argument.

I went into an empty apartment. On the refrigerator door was a note from my mother.

Cath—

 John and I went to a lecture at the University. We'll probably be back about eleven. Hope you had a good time with your father. Remember that he does *love you very much.*

         Love,
         Mom

At that particular moment, it was hard to see the love in what Dad was doing.

Chapter Twelve

You know, life sure would be a lot easier to manage if problems came one at a time. I mean, I could possibly manage dealing with my father *or* with Tony *or* with Bulldozer Boy. Instead, I was mixed up about all three of them simultaneously, only to have Mary drop *her* bombshell on me. Suddenly I felt like there was an absolute conspiracy afoot to drive me stark raving mad. Let's see—Cath is only completely boggled; let's have a crisis with her best friend and see if she really goes over the edge. I'm sure I sound paranoid, but that truly was how I felt.

You have to understand Mary. Normally, Mary is the most energetic, enthusiastic, high-spirited, confident person I know. Sure, there are times when she gets depressed, especially about things like her grandfather being really sick, and there are plenty of times when she gets mad—like at Mark about every other day. When I think of Mary, though, I never see her like that. I see her with her head thrown back, laughing at some silly joke, reaching out to include everyone around her in her laughter. Perhaps it is the old theory that opposites attract. I'm the one on the fringes, enjoying the laughter but not wanting to be the center of it, while Mary loves to have all eyes on her. Whatever the reason, we have been best friends since we were little kids, and I can't visualize my life without Mary as a part of it.

I went to school the day after my big argument with my father all ready to talk to Mary about it. Granted, Mary's mother and father still seem happily married so she doesn't know what it's like to go through divorce and all that follows, but she still was the person I most wanted to talk to about my father. I knew Mary would listen, and I knew she would give me her opinion no matter whether I would like it or not. If she thought I was overreacting, she would tell me; if she thought my father was being a jerk, she'd tell me that too. Mary believed that friends should be honest and she was, sometimes brutally so.

I waited until lunch when we had a solid half hour to talk. I met her at our regular table in the cafeteria, glad to see that both of us had brown paper bags on top of our books so we wouldn't have to waste time waiting in the lunch line to buy platters. The second I went to sit down, though, Mary spoke.

"Cath, we have to get out of here. I can't stand it here. I simply cannot stand it. We have to get out. Now. Right now. I'm not kidding, Cath."

Good heavens, I thought, looking around. The cafeteria certainly was not the most elegant place I'd ever seen, but it didn't seem to deserve this kind of high drama. The rising hysteria in Mary's voice left me no choice, however. With every declaration her voice was getting louder and louder. Soon the entire student body would be staring at us.

"Okay, okay. Calm down," I said. "Where do you want to go?"

"Anywhere but here. I can't breathe. I'm going to throw up if I don't get out of here."

Once again the hysteria was rising. "Let's go," I said quickly, grabbing my books and my lunch bag.

73

We dashed for the nearest doorway. Once we were in the hall, I couldn't figure out where to go. Finally, inspiration struck. In the far back corner of the library there was a conference room. With any luck it would be empty and we would have a quiet place to talk. I steered Mary in that direction. The librarian was occupied behind the desk, and we quickly walked to the conference room, Mary following me blindly. Students weren't supposed to be in the conference room without a teacher, but the door was unlocked and we went in, shutting the door quietly behind us. Mary immediately sat down on the floor, ignoring the chairs that surrounded the large circular table. Not knowing what else to do, I sat on the floor beside her.

Silence followed. Minute after minute after minute of silence. At first I thought I would wait her out, but after all, lunch only lasted for thirty minutes. I decided I'd have to speed up the process. "Mary, what's wrong? Are you sick? Did you have another fight with Mark? Is your grandfather worse? Did your parents ground you?" Each question went unanswered. This wasn't like Mary. Out of those four possibilities, one of them should have at least gotten some kind of response. "Mary, talk to me. You rush me out of the cafeteria as if the world is ending, and now you won't even talk to me. That's not fair."

"Cath, I think I'm pregnant." That certainly shut me up. In fact, I felt like I might not ever speak again. What do you say to your best friend in the whole world when she says that? All I could think was, I didn't even think she'd done IT yet. Wasn't that ironic, going back to our uncomfortable childhood expression for sex—IT. Meanwhile, the silence grew.

"Cath, say something. Say you hate me, say you think I'm a horrible, evil person, say you think I'm a sleazeball, but say something." Her voice was rising

74

again, and I had visions of the librarian coming to hover outside the conference room door.

"Mary, I don't hate you. I'm just surprised, to put it mildly. Give me a chance to get used to the idea." I might as well say, give me a year or two.

"I don't want to get used to the idea. I don't want to be pregnant. I can't believe this is happening."

I couldn't believe it either, but I didn't think I'd better spend much time worrying about how I felt. Mary needed to be calmed down, and fast. "Maybe you'd better start at the beginning. When did you and Mark . . ." I paused, but maturity won out, even though I didn't like the sound of the words ". . . have sex?"

"Yesterday," was Mary's prompt answer.

I laughed. Unfortunately, I laughed out loud, and Mary was not pleased. I knew it wasn't funny, but still, it broke the horrible tension in that conference room. "I'm sorry, Mary. I'm not laughing at you, at least I don't mean to. I know that none of this is funny. But if you only had sex yesterday, how can you know you're pregnant already?"

"I just know it, Cath. I feel sick, really sick, and I *deserve* to be pregnant for being so stupid. I can't believe I let this happen."

I was puzzled. As well as I know Mary, she'd left me behind in her logic. I tried to sort it out. "Mary, even if you are pregnant, I don't think the morning sickness starts the first day, does it?"

"How am I supposed to know? I've never been maybe pregnant before." Again I almost laughed, but this time I stopped before any noise came out.

"Mary, I think you might be sick because you're so tense. Remember that time before the school play?"

That got a smile even from Mary. She had been the star of a play that our class put on in seventh grade. Before the play began she was so nervous that she threw up about four times. After the play ended, she had cried because she loved the applause and she couldn't stand to think that it was over. I'd never let her live down that particular evening.

"This is different, Cath. That was excited sick. This is scared sick."

"Let's not jump to any conclusions. Everything might be fine. Don't panic—at least not yet." Actually, I was starting to panic at the thought that Mary might be pregnant, and that must be a very mild form of what Mary was feeling. Poor Mary—but then a new idea started to grow in my head. Poor Mary? What had she done to get herself in this predicament? "Mary, I don't mean to pry, but . . ."

She interrupted before I had to finish the sentence. "I know, Cath, and I don't blame you for thinking I'm stupid. I know it was just a couple of months ago that we talked about not being ready to have sex yet, and I wasn't, I mean I wasn't then, but last night things just got carried away."

"It sure sounds like it," I said, and Mary looked at me searchingly to see if I was being snide. I wasn't.

"Mark and I went to the library to study. Cath, don't look at me that way. We really did go to study, and we *did* study, but then I got bored and hungry so we went to McDonalds to get french fries."

So far that made sense. French fries were Mary's answer to most problems in life—except this one.

"Then Mark drove down to Creek Road."

"Uh oh," I said. Creek Road is notorious as a place to go parking. The road is twisty and narrow and dark, and it winds around near the Brandywine River. There are some places where cars can pull off the road, and those places are famous among high-school students. In fact, Creek Road was a legend with both Mary's mother and mine. We had been warned and threatened and begged to stay away from there since before either of us had ever had a boyfriend to consider taking us there.

"And we were sitting in the car, and the moon was full and shining off the river, and it was so quiet and peaceful, and we were just talking."

"Mary!" I said. "Come on, now. Be serious." After all, just talking didn't create this kind of problem.

"Okay, then we stopped talking, and Mark was kissing me and holding me, and I felt so close to him that it seemed like anything we did would be okay." Mary looked at me pleadingly, and I bit back the words I was almost ready to say. "I know, Cath," she said quietly. "It's not like I made a conscious decision— okay, I'm going to let Mark make love to me. I didn't decide. I just didn't stop him. I just let what happened happen. I know that doesn't make sense to you. It doesn't even make sense to me now. But at the time everything that Mark did to me felt gentle and loving and good, and I didn't want to think. I just wanted to feel. Then by the time I realized that I really should be doing something to stop it, it seemed too late. Then it just didn't seem fair to Mark to stop when I'd let it get that far. He meant to stop, he kept saying that he would after just one more second, one more, but he didn't."

"Neither of you used any kind of protection?"

"No, Cath. I know how stupid it sounds now, but I just didn't think about it. If I had, we wouldn't have made love. I didn't plan on it happening, and if I'd stopped to make a logical decision, I would have decided not to do it."

That sort of made sense to me, but it sure didn't help the situation.

"I know I'm pregnant," Mary repeated. "It's my punishment for being so stupid. It's not like I didn't take Health in ninth grade. It's not like my parents haven't had talks with me. I'm not sure I was even really ready to have sex, let alone have a baby."

"How's Mark dealing with all of this?" I asked. After all, Mary hadn't been at Creek Road alone.

"He's trying to pretend it never happened, but I think he's scared, too. He'd better be."

I hoped Mary was right. All she needed was for Mark to act like a macho jerk, bragging to his friends.

With that, the bell rang. At least Mary seemed a tiny bit calmer. Of course, now I was a nervous wreck, too. We walked to our classes in silence.

My mind was in a fog, but one thought penetrated. Mary had said that I wouldn't understand how she felt. She was wrong. Sometimes that's exactly how Tony'd made me feel.

Chapter Thirteen

I don't think either Mary or I got any sleep that night. The next day we both stumbled into school, red-eyed and pale. During lunch, however, we snuck back into the conference room and made some decisions. Actually, we made a list—or rather, I made a list. Somehow life seems easier to manage when things are numbered.

1. Don't panic. Both of us need to continue leading lives that are as normal as possible. After all, there might not *be* a problem.

2. Don't tell either Mary's parents or mine—yet, at least. (Actually, all I had to think about was my mother. Could you see telling my *father*? He already thought I was living in an immoral environment. Somehow I didn't think a pregnant best friend would please him terribly.)

3. Do some research. (We both knew that Mary had had sex, but what were the odds that she was pregnant?)

4. Make sure that Mark was just as worried as Mary. (Somehow this seemed very important to both of us.)

5. Don't do anything crazy.

This was definitely directed at Mary. It was added to the list after Mary confessed that she had spent the previous night considering the following:

—joining a nunnery and then claiming that the baby was a miracle from God;

—running away to Alaska where there are a lot of men for every woman and some man would be so glad for female companionship that he would take in both Mary and her baby-to-be without making any demands whatsoever;

—killing herself by stealing Mark's car and crashing it on Creek Road so that Mark would feel horribly guilty forever and would never again be capable of having sex because he would always remember Mary's terrible fate.

Once our list was done, there was only one item that I could be of much help with, and that was doing research. Unfortunately, that turned out to be a little more difficult than it seemed. By the time we had finished our list, there were only a few minutes left of lunch. Still, we decided to start. Surely a high-school library would have books that would help. First we went to the card catalog.

"What should we look up?" Mary asked.

"Pregnancy," I replied.

"Will you be quiet?" Mary practically screamed. "Don't use that word in public."

I wanted to say, "Mary, if you are, more than the word is going to be noticed in public," but I didn't. Instead, all I said was "Fine. What's your suggestion?"

"Sex," Mary announced.

"Great," I replied. "Let's broadcast it over the loudspeaker." Actually, our voices were causing heads to turn.

A search under "Sex" in the card catalog turned up some promising titles, and a dash to the shelves found two or three. Mary piled them in her arms and started toward the sign-out desk, then abruptly stopped, almost making me crash into her.

"What's wrong with you?" I asked.

"I can't sign these out," she said in a horrified tone of voice.

"Why? Don't you have your ID with you?"

"No, it's not that. She'll know."

I looked at Mary in amazement. "Who will know what?"

"The librarian. Once she sees what books I'm signing out, she'll know I'm pregnant."

"Mary, *you* don't even know if you're pregnant. She'll just think you're doing research."

"Research for what? Cath, I can't go up there with these books. She'll know, and she'll call my mother."

Now I knew how ridiculous that last part was, but I could hear the hysteria rising in Mary's voice again. "Mary, just sign them out. If you're worried, say it's for a research paper. You're being silly."

"If I'm being silly, then you sign them out." Mary stared at me defiantly.

"Fine. I will." Before I could say anything more, Mary dumped the books in my arms, smashing my uneaten lunch in the process. I looked at the titles: *Sex and the Teenager. So You're Young and Pregnant— What Next? Contraception and You.* Suddenly Mary didn't seem so silly any more. "You're right. I don't feel right about it either." We stuck the books back on the shelf just as the bell rang. As it was, the librarian gave us a slightly puzzled look.

Our research continued after school. This time we decided to forget the school library and go to the library downtown. I drove there in the red VW, turning on the radio to fill the silence Mary left. As we walked in, I tried to lighten Mary's mood. "If you'd only decided to stay here and study rather than ending up

on Creek Road, none of this would have happened."
Mary failed to see any humor in that. In fact, for a
moment I thought she was going to slug me.

We were getting better at finding the right section in
the card catalog, and we had already looked to see who
was working at the checkout desk. It was a relatively
young woman neither of us knew. This would work.
We found the right shelves and began to choose books
on sex and pregnancy.

"Mary! I do declare! What a nice surprise seeing
you here in the library. And isn't that Cath Berry with
you? Cath, how *is* your mother? I think it is just grand
that she picked herself right up and got that nice law
degree after your father left her."

If Mary and I had bad hearts, we would have been
dead. There we were, concentrating on our research,
when the shrill, piercing voice of Mrs. Hartsong sent
us practically jumping to the ceiling. Mrs. Hartsong is,
without a doubt, the biggest gossip in Delaware. One
never has a conversation with her—it's an interroga-
tion. Besides, she knows everyone in town. I think I
finally figured out how she does it. Whenever she is
talking to one person, she is constantly asking, "Now
who's that?" or, "Just who was that long-haired girl
I saw you walking down Main Street with yesterday?" or, "Don't you have an uncle who used to date
a cousin of that girl who works in the pharmacy
at Happy Harry's?" Her sphere of knowledge is
constantly widening, like ripples radiating outward
from a disturbance in water.

Anyway, of all the people Mary and I needed to see
at that particular moment, Mrs. Hartsong was near the
bottom of the list. I could just hear it now. "Oh, Mrs.
Berry. How wonderful it is that Cath and her little
friend Mary are such bookworms. Why just yesterday

I ran into them browsing in the sex and pregnancy section of the library." Great.

Mary looked like she was either going to pass out or throw up. I decided I'd better do something fast. "Why, Mrs. Hartsong. How nice to see you. I'm afraid my mother is expecting me home soon, so we're in a rush. Now where would that new novel by Robert Parker be? Oh Mary, look! Silly us! We're in the nonfiction section by mistake. The novels are over *there*." Still babbling like an idiot, I shoved Mary down the aisle. I didn't know if Mrs. Hartsong bought the act or not, and I couldn't risk looking back to find out. All I could hope was that instead of telling our mothers we were checking out sex and pregnancy books, she would tell them that they had raised idiot daughters who didn't know the Dewey decimal system.

After a thirty-second search of the fiction shelves, I steered Mary toward the door. Mrs. Hartsong was still watching us. "Just can't keep those Parker novels on the shelves," I said as we rushed out.

Once outside, Mary regained a little color. Of course, an additional problem remained—we still didn't have any books. I could think of only one more possibility, so I drove toward Main Street and the bookstore. By the time I parked the car, Mary and I were searching the vicinity like spies. We looked up and down Main Street, even checking out who was in the passing cars. I halfway expected to see Mrs. Hartsong come sprinting down the street. We didn't see anyone we knew, but still we both remained tense and alert. The next major hurdle was entering the bookstore. That wasn't too bad. After all, we could still look like innocent girls searching for the latest best-seller. Without even saying anything, Mary and I split off in different directions as soon as we entered the store. She searched one half; I searched the other. We met in the middle after both of us had stared at the salesclerk.

"Strangers," Mary said. "Everyone in here is a stranger to me."

"Nobody familiar to me either," I said, feeling slightly ridiculous.

"Do you think any of these people know our mothers?" Mary asked.

"Now how am I supposed to know?" I asked. "Shall we ask them?"

"No," Mary practically screamed. "No," she repeated more quietly. "I think it's safe."

Then we made the next big move—the one that took us to the sex and pregnancy section. By now we could practically home in on those books. Once again we searched, this time narrowing it down to just one book—*Fertility and Contraception*. That seemed like it would cover what we wanted to know. Every ten seconds or so, one of us would wheel around looking for Mrs. Hartsong.

I made Mary carry the book up to the cash register, even though she wanted me to. Then the final disaster struck. Mary began searching frantically through her pocketbook. As the clerk watched in amazement, she dumped makeup, keys, one dirty sweatsock, three lint-covered lifesavers, and her notes from history class onto the counter. "I know I have money in here," she muttered. "I have a five dollar bill." She dumped her pocketbook upside down, but all that rolled out was seventeen cents. "Oh, I remember now," she finally said to the shell-shocked clerk. "I treated at McDonalds night before last."

Great, I thought. She paid for the french fries that led away from the library and to Creek Road. She must have even paid for Mark's food so that he could have plenty of energy for the grand seduction. While I thought all of this, I was searching through my pocketbook. I added a receipt from the dry cleaners, bonus stamps from the grocery store, my savings account book, and about ten notes from Mary to the pile on the counter. In the process I found four dollars and ninety cents.

The clerk must have felt like he had been invaded by a traveling flea market. "The book is $5.50," he said with a slight sneer, "and we don't accept sweatsocks."

Mary never ceases to amaze me. Instead of blushing and wanting to disappear under the floorboards, she stared right into the clerk's eyes. "I don't think I like your attitude," she said in a controlled, haughty voice. With that she swept all of her belongings back into her pocketbook, and I did the same. Out we walked.

Neither of us had the nerve to face any more research. I dropped Mary off at her house and then fled to the relative sanity of our apartment. I had the distinct feeling that some day that afternoon would seem very funny, but neither Mary or I was laughing yet.

Chapter Fourteen

Making Mark miserable became one of my major goals. After all, had he spent all kinds of time trying to research pregnancy? Was he lying awake at night worrying as much as Mary was? I somehow didn't think he was, and that made me furious.

The next day, I saw him at school before seventh period, leaning against the wall, laughing and joking with the guys. I wanted to kick him. I wanted to see shadows under his eyes, lines of worry etched across his forehead. I wanted him to be sneaking around in libraries, being startled by Mrs. Hartsong, and I wanted him to pay for *Fertility and Contraception*. Since I didn't think I could achieve all that, I decided on a little dose of guilt.

"Hi, Mark," I said in a very subdued tone. My face was somber, my shoulders slumped.

"What's wrong with you?" Mark asked brightly. "You look like your best friend just died."

That was definitely a bad choice of words for him. "Well, she might as well have, considering the problem she might be facing."

With that, I wheeled away from him and stalked down the hallway, taking just long enough to enjoy the startled look on his face. After all, Mark must have been in a somewhat awkward position. He knew that Mary and I were very close friends, but I bet he was counting on Mary not telling *anybody* about what had happened. Wrong, Mark.

Happy that I had given him a little something to think about, I went into Spanish class. As usual, Bulldozer Boy was in his corner seat. I went to my seat in the front row but Mr. Anderson called out, "Dialogues today, Cath," so I picked up my books again and went back to sit next to Bulldozer Boy. My working with him had become routine. Mr. Anderson always made me his partner, and there was nothing I could do about it. Actually it wasn't so bad. Bulldozer Boy had an excellent command of Spanish, better than mine, so writing with him was easy. After a while, the silence had become normal to me, almost comfortable. When the time came to read the dialogues out loud, Mr. Anderson always read the second part with me. It wasn't so bad. Even the other kids had pretty much stopped joking about it. They had learned to enjoy the wit in our dialogues, and I think they knew that it must be coming from Bulldozer Boy, not me.

Anyway, as soon as I sat down next to Bulldozer Boy, I knew there was a problem. Much was the same—his turquoise eyes were still darting around, his hair was still uncombed, and his same brown jacket still surrounded him. The difference was the blood. There was a small but nasty-looking cut over his left eye, and blood was steadily dripping from it, making a small red pool on the desk.

"You're bleeding," I yelped, and he turned to look at me. He didn't say anything, but his eyes stared at me as if they were willing me to be quiet. Now that was something I understood. If I didn't like attention, think how he must feel.

Quickly I went to Mr. Anderson's desk. He had a large box of tissues, and I grabbed a handful. Mr. Anderson looked at me questioningly but didn't say anything. I went back to Bulldozer Boy and held out the tissues. He wasn't looking at me, and he didn't take them. He was facing away from me when I touched his arm, merely wanting to get his attention. At the touch, he wheeled around toward me with amazing speed, fists raised. His eyes blazed with fierce energy, and I thought he was going to attack me.

"Hey—I just wanted to give you these. I didn't mean to startle you." My words seemed to penetrate, and slowly the tension went out of him. I breathed for the first time in half a minute or so. Once again I held out the tissues. His eyes met mine, and then he turned away again. Still the blood dripped.

"Look, maybe you don't mind, but I find it hard to concentrate on writing a dialogue when your blood is dripping all over the table."

He turned back to me, and there was almost a trace of a smile on his face. I held the wad of tissues up to his head, absorbing the blood, then wiped up most of what was on the desk. As soon as I took the padding away, however, blood started to flow again. This was simply not going to do. Besides, why was this boy bleeding? That was not a superficial scratch that was causing all of this mess. What had happened to Bulldozer Boy?

So far this medical emergency had gotten little attention from the rest of the class since the kids were all busy arranging themselves into pairs to settle into work. It was inevitable, however, that someone would notice the blood soon. Sure we were back in the far corner, but still blood was hard to miss for long, and it was continuing to drip from Bulldozer Boy's head at a rate that was starting to alarm me.

"Here. Hold this. Apply pressure." I jammed the tissues against his head. Luckily, this time he did cooperate by holding them in place when I removed my hand. "I'll be right back."

Mr. Anderson was sitting at his desk grading papers. As I walked toward him, I started to get angry. After all, he was the teacher, and if a student was bleeding in his room, *he* should have to deal with it, not me. Somehow, though, I knew that he had turned Bulldozer Boy over to me. Swell.

"Mr. Anderson, Bull . . . Robert seems to have a cut over his eye. May I please have a pass to the nurse for both of us?"

Mr. Anderson looked up in surprise. He looked back toward the corner, but Bulldozer Boy was angled away from him.

"Trust me, he's bleeding all over the desk. I'll take care of it. Just write us a pass."

Quickly Mr. Anderson rummaged through his desk drawer, found the proper form, and wrote down the proper information. "Do you want me to call the office or . . ."

"No, I think I can handle it. I'll let you know if there's any problem."

"Thanks, Cath. Don't worry about the dialogue. You can have an extra day to turn it in if you need it." With one more worried glance toward the back of the room, he went back to grading.

The man was all heart. I went back to Bulldozer Boy and gathered together his books and mine. "Come on. We're going to the nurse."

He looked at me, then turned away.

Great, I thought. Now what am I going to do? Let him bleed to death?

"I want you to come with me. You can't just sit there and bleed. I won't let you. Now get up before we make a big scene." I was hissing the words at him in a nasty whisper. For a moment I thought he was going to call my bluff. After all, what could I do? There was a considerable size difference, and I didn't exactly love the idea of trying to physically drag him out of the classroom. I looked toward the front of the room and saw Mr. Anderson watching us. The minute my eyes met his, he turned back to his grading.

"Move." I got up and headed for the door, praying that he was following me. I didn't look back until I was out in the hallway. Luckily for me, there came Bulldozer Boy.

"Come on. Let's go to the nurse. You probably need ice or stitches or something." The nurse's office was down the hallway to the left, and that was the way I headed. Bulldozer Boy took off toward the right. It seemed like my luck had suddenly ended again. He was gaining momentum with every step, and I had to break into a run to catch up with him. That wasn't especially easy considering how fast he moved and how many books I was carrying. I caught up with him as he headed out the door at the end of the hallway.

"Will you wait a minute? For one thing, I have your books, and I have no desire to carry them around for you." That seemed to get his attention, and he stopped outside the door. There was a stairwell with steps that led out to a small strip of grass and the faculty parking lot.

"I take it this means you don't want to go to the nurse." I sat on the top step, tired and frustrated. Bulldozer Boy sat down next to me. The tissues were now red all the way through with blood.

"Look, I don't think it's good to lose this much blood. I really wish you'd go to the nurse." He started to get up, so I abruptly reconsidered. "Of course, if you don't want to do that, maybe it would be good just to sit here for a moment."

At least he seemed willing to do that. I rummaged

through my pocketbook and found some more tissues. I folded them into a thick square and handed them to him. "Now apply as much pressure as you can." He put his elbow on his knee, then leaned his head on his hand. I guessed that would do. I searched my brain for whatever first aid I knew. I remembered hearing about applying pressure and about tying something tight between a bleeding wound and the heart. Great. If his head was bleeding, did I have to tie off his neck? I had never considered nursing as a profession, and this was reinforcing that decision. Besides, the sight of blood was making my stomach turn.

"How did you get that cut?" I don't know why I asked; after all, the odds were excellent that he wouldn't answer. I decided to try some yes-no questions. "Did you run into something?" He looked at me as if I were crazy. I decided to take that as a no.

"Were you in an accident on the way to school today?"

Again I got a look of scorn.

"Did someone hit you?" Considering how he was treated around school, that suddenly seemed like it must be the answer. Bulldozer Boy turned away at that question, refusing to meet my eyes. I took that as a yes. The only thing that still confused me was who— and with what. The cut over his eye was not the type that results from being punched. There didn't seem to be much bruising or swelling, at least not that I could see.

"What were you hit with?" Still he remained turned around. I leaned almost across him, trying to see his eyes, trying to read some kind of response. At my movement he started to get up and I could sense that he was ready to bolt away from me again. I moved away from him, left him plenty of space, and he sat again, still tense but at least motionless.

"Who did this? I know that kids tease you, but this is going too far. You should report this to your advisor. Whoever did this shouldn't get away with it." I was getting wound up. After all, there was a lot of blood flowing, and even if Bulldozer Boy was strange, he didn't deserve to bleed to death for it.

"Who did this? If you won't go to the nurse, let's go to your advisor." This time I did get a response— of sorts. Bulldozer Boy half snorted, half laughed. It was actually a very sad sound. It was filled with resignation. He seemed to be scoffing at the idea that anyone would help him. Of course, if I'd had as many problems at school as he'd had, I probably wouldn't exactly trust the system either.

Another thought darted into my mind. "Well, if you don't want any help from the school, at least your parents are going to be pretty mad about this. I bet they'll be on the phone to the principal the minute they see your head. I know my mother sure would be."

Obviously I had said the wrong thing. Bulldozer Boy looked at me, and I felt like all the sorrow in the world was in his eyes. For what felt like an eternity, he stared at me, and there was pain in that look, and something that went deeper than pain. Then he was gone. Before I could say another word or try to stop him or even try to follow him, he was gone. He was across the grass, between the cars, and out of sight. I stared after him in amazement. What had I said? What had I done?

I felt cold. I hadn't noticed how chilly the air was. For a moment I couldn't decide what to do. A look at my watch showed about twenty minutes left of seventh period. Should I go back to Mr. Anderson and tell him that I had lost Bulldozer Boy? After all, I wasn't where I'd said I would be, but there didn't seem to be much use in going to the nurse's office without the person who needed the medical help. Somehow, though, I didn't think Mr. Anderson was going to write me up for cutting class. Did he want to explain why he hadn't done anything about a bleeding student? Finally, I simply didn't decide on anything. I just sat on the step, cold and confused.

What was happening? Why was I even concerned about Bulldozer Boy? It was funny how I had completely forgotten the injuries *he* had caused *me* on the first day of school. At least I hadn't lost any blood. Who had done that to him? Why wouldn't he talk? Could he talk if he wanted to?

I came up with no answers, only more questions. Finally I heard the dismissal bell ring, and I blended into the crowd that rushed out the door. It was only when the pile of books in my arms seemed unusually heavy that I remembered that I still had Bulldozer Boy's.

Chapter Fifteen

I waited at my car after school that day, looking around for Bulldozer Boy and looking also for Mary. I was pretty sure I wouldn't find Bulldozer Boy. When he had run away from me, he hadn't looked like he'd be back in the near future. I thought that maybe he had to come back to catch a bus, but somehow I didn't think that was likely. A bus ride would be a nightmare for him—closed up in a small area with people who would probably torment him nonstop. My chances of finding Mary were better. At lunch she'd said that she didn't feel good and that she might go home early. If she didn't, however, she'd said she'd meet me at my car after school.

Sure enough, I had only been sitting in the VW a few minutes when I saw Mary walking across the parking lot toward me. She was walking slowly, without the customary bounce in her step. She threw herself into the passenger's seat, heaving her books onto the floor in the back.

"Are you feeling better?" She looked pale.

"Not really, but I didn't want the nurse to be suspicious of me." Mary's paranoia was growing by the day.

"Do you think it might be better to just tell your parents so you can stop worrying about someone else doing it?"

"Cath, how can you even suggest such a thing?" Mary was staring at me in amazement, and I was almost afraid that she was going to bolt out of the car. I seemed to have developed a talent for saying the worst possible thing at the worst possible moment.

"Sorry, Mary. It's just that you know your parents love you, and no matter how upset they'd be, you know they would help you."

"Sure, after they got done crying and screaming and blaming themselves and blaming Mark and grounding me until I'm ready for menopause."

"Mary, you're driving yourself crazy. You can't live like this."

"How would you like me to live?"

"Let's just try to get some answers. I have money today. We'll go back to the bookstore."

I got no answer from Mary, just a sigh. I took that as a yes, and drove back down to Main Street. I found a parking space right in front of the bookstore, got out, put a nickel in the meter, and started in the door before I realized that Mary wasn't with me. I looked back and there she was, slumped down in the seat, staring straight ahead. I walked back to the car and tapped on the window. She refused to look at me.

I leaned down and talked to her through the glass. "Come on, Mary. We need to buy the book."

No answer. She kept looking straight ahead, eyes glazed.

"Roll down the window." No response. "Mary, this isn't funny. We need answers. We need that book. Now come on."

Not only was there no answer, but a man walking by on the sidewalk was giving me a very strange look.

"Fine. I'll do it myself." I marched into the bookstore, found *Fertility and Contraception*, took out six dollars, and went to the counter. Luckily it was a different clerk from the one we'd dealt with before. This one took my money, put the book in a bag, and gave me my change. I refused to meet his eyes, so I don't know if he was looking at me suspiciously or not. He started to say something, but I was out the door before the end of the first syllable.

When I got to the car, I threw open the door and then slammed it shut. I hurled the bag at Mary, started the engine, and gunned it loudly. I pulled out into a small break in the traffic, causing the car behind me to throw on its brakes. I finally calmed down, reasoning that crashing the car would punish me more than it would Mary. I started to drive toward her house, then changed my mind and headed toward our apartment. Mary's mother didn't work, and chances were good she would be home. There was no chance my mother and Mr. Donelly would be home for hours yet.

Mary was silent all the way home, all the way into the apartment, and all the way to my room, where she finally fell across my bed. I got her a glass of root beer, which she ignored. The book was still in its bag. I picked it up and went to my rocking chair by the window. I started reading.

"That's interesting," I said after about five minutes of reading. "Uh-oh," I said after several more minutes.

"What?" Mary finally said. I knew that she'd break down sooner or later. No matter how upset or depressed Mary was, she couldn't keep quiet indefinitely. I mean, this was a girl who *always* got "Socializing interferes with learning" on the comment section of her report card.

"Why did you say 'uh-oh?' "

"Just to get your attention."

"Cath! Don't joke about this. I can't stand it."

I took the book over to her, and we studied it together. As nearly as we could tell, she definitely could be pregnant but it was also possible that she wasn't. According to the book, she had had sex at the end of her fertile time of month, not at the absolutely most dangerous time. Still, there was a definite risk.

"Cath," Mary finally said, quietly and firmly, "I just want you to know one thing. I am never, and I mean never, going to have sex again. There is no way it is worth all of this."

"Never?" I asked. "Not even on your wedding night?"

"Not even then," she replied.

"Do you plan to explain this to your husband-to-be in advance?"

"No. I think I'll just let it be a surprise. Serve him right. Men. I hate them all."

I laughed, but Mary didn't join in. At least she didn't hit me for laughing, though.

Based on what we now knew, we came up with a plan. If Mary wasn't pregnant, we'd probably know within about another week. If not, we decided we'd buy one of those home pregnancy detection kits. I could see it now—whatever drugstore we went to, there would be Mrs. Hartsong and every other person either of our mothers knew. We'd probably have to drive to New Jersey before we'd be sure that we wouldn't be seen.

"Yes, and wear disguises," Mary added when I told her what I'd been thinking.

"And this time *you're* going in. There is no way I'm doing it for you."

"Thanks, Cath. I just couldn't move."

"It's okay."

We also agreed that if the results were positive, we would then go to a Planned Parenthood clinic. Of course, we'd probably have to go to North Carolina before we'd feel safe walking into one of those.

"Mary, maybe Mark should go, not me."

"Cath, you're not going to abandon me, are you? Promise you won't abandon me."

"I just don't want Mark to abandon you," I said, "and I think we'd make a rather confusing threesome."

"He wouldn't understand. He probably wouldn't even wear a disguise."

"We'll worry about that when and if we need to. Just calm down, Mary."

I knew that was easy for me to say, but she needed to get a grip. "I know, Cath, and I'm trying. Really I am. You'd better take me home. I don't want to have to answer questions from my mother." Mary started out of my bedroom.

"Here. You forgot the book." I started to toss it to her.

"I can't take it with me. My mother might find it."

"So you want to leave it here for *my* mother to find? Mary!"

"Cath, your mother trusts you more than my mother trusts me, so she's a lot less likely to search your room than mine is."

I had to admit that my mother was good about leaving my room alone.

"We'll find a good hiding place." Mary started to prowl around my room. "Here. We'll put it under the mattress." She did so, leaving a noticeable lump in my bed.

"Mary, I don't think so."

"Don't be so picky. Okay, how about here?" She stuck the book onto the bookshelf above my desk. The red letters of *Fertility and Contraception* seemed to glow in neon between *The Little Prince* and *The Catcher in the Rye*.

"Give it here," I said. I opened my closet door, rummaged for a moment, then stuck the book in the pocket of a terry cloth robe hanging in the back.

"Brilliant," Mary proclaimed.

"Only in comparison to your choices," I said.

"I really think you should take me home," Mary said.

It sounded like a good idea. Heaven only knew what she'd be asking me to do next.

I dropped Mary off in front of her house, then returned home once again. With a sigh of relief, I headed for my room, ready to curl up with a good mystery book. Maybe a twisted plot would take my mind off Mary's problems. I had just opened the Robert Ludlum book that had finally come out in paperback when the doorbell rang. I seriously considered not answering the door, but I decided I'd better.

"Angela Berry?" inquired the man at the door.

"No, but I'm her daughter."

"These are for Angela Berry." Suddenly I was holding a long box from Taylor's Florist Shop. The man looked at me inquiringly, then shook his head and left. Only when he was down the steps did I realize that I probably should have tipped him.

I took the box into the kitchen and untied the ribbon. After all, the flowers might need water. Inside the box were six long-stemmed red roses surrounded by baby's breath and ferns. Tiny drops of water misted the brilliant crimson petals. They were so beautiful that I could hardly bear to touch them. I looked at the clock. Mom wouldn't be home for another hour or two, so I decided I'd better put them in water. I found our best crystal vase and arranged them in it. Then I put the flowers on the dining room table where Mom would be certain to see them as soon as she came in. There was a small card tucked into an envelope, and I put that in front of the roses. It wasn't sealed, and for a moment I considered peeking.

"No," I said to myself. "If Mom doesn't snoop in my room, I can't snoop in her envelopes."

Besides, I was sure they must be from Mr. Donelly. After all, who else would send my mother roses?

Chapter Sixteen

Mom and Mr. Donelly got home around 6:30, just as I was finally immersed in the Ludlum novel, worrying about counter-espionage instead of Mary. I could hear Mom's voice from the dining room.

"These roses are gorgeous. Cath, who sent them?"

Regretfully I shut my book and went out to see my mother. "I don't know. They're for you." She looked from me back to the roses, her expression quizzical. Then she looked at Mr. Donelly.

"John! You shouldn't have! What's the occasion?"

"I wish I could claim the credit for these, but I can't." Mr. Donelly sounded both apologetic and suspicious.

"Mom, will you open the envelope? I can't stand the suspense." I'd just been reading a spy novel and I had a maybe-pregnant friend. I didn't need to wonder about anything more.

Mom ripped open the envelope. "Why, they're from your father!" she said in surprise.

"What does the card say?" I asked.

Mom held it away from me, but that only put it closer to Mr. Donelly. He was polite enough not to grab for it. Finally Mom held it out to me.

"Happy Anniversary. William." That was all it said. After I had read the words, silence descended. It was Mom who finally broke it.

"I truly had forgotten that today is—would be—my wedding anniversary," she said.

"Obviously your husband—or should I say ex-husband—hasn't forgotten," Mr. Donelly replied. His eyebrow was twitching. I honestly felt sorry for him, so I tried to help.

"Mom, maybe it's his way of apologizing for the trouble he's caused since he came back from Saudi Arabia. You know, trying to get me to live with him and saying you're immoral and all."

From the looks on both faces, I hadn't done a very good job of helping.

Finally Mom said, "Maybe you're right, Cath, but if he wanted to apologize, he could have found a more appropriate way, and he should have included you in the apology."

"Well, give me three of the roses," I said. Mom did exactly that. She pulled out three of the roses and handed them to me.

"I don't want them," I said with a laugh, sticking them back in the vase. "It was just a test."

"Did I pass?" Mom asked.

"Of course," I answered. "You always do."

"I think that William has a different test in mind," said Mr. Donelly.

Mom looked at him questioningly. "What test is that?"

"I think he's trying to re-establish his claim on you."

"His claim on me?" Mom asked in disbelief. "What claim? We're divorced and have been for many years now. The only claim he has on me is the one created by Cath, and he knows that."

"Does he?" asked Mr. Donelly.

"Why wouldn't he?" Mom replied.

"You tell me," said Mr. Donelly, and he stomped

off to the bedroom. Actually, stomped is too strong a word for Mr. Donelly, but he did walk more heavily than usual.

"I don't believe this," said Mom, sitting down at the dining room table.

"I think it's kind of cute," I said.

"Cath, what do you mean?"

"Well, I've never seen Mr. Donelly act like a jealous boyfriend before."

"Jealous? Of your father? Are you crazy?"

"Now Mom, obviously there was something that attracted you to my father. You *did* marry him, and you *did* have me."

Now it was my mother's turn to be flustered. "Of course I was attracted to your father. I loved your father, very much as a matter of fact."

"So now Mr. Donelly is jealous of that."

"But I don't love your father any more. That's part of a former life, a person I used to be. I moved on from that."

The phone interrupted before she could say anything else. We looked at each other.

"If that's your father, tell him I'm not home."

"Mom, you're not supposed to ask me to lie."

"Cath, answer the phone."

"Yes, Mother," I said, sickeningly sweet. She laughed.

"Hello?"

"Cath? This is David. I'm sorry to call you at the last minute, but I'm at work at the grocery store and a guy I work with needs tomorrow off instead of today and that means he'll work for me tonight if I'll work for him tomorrow." Then there was a pause.

"That's nice," I finally said. Why was he telling me this?

"I know it's short notice, but would you like to go

102

to a movie tonight? I could go home, change, and pick you up in about an hour.''

The idea of getting out of this madhouse where my mother, her current boyfriend, and her ex-husband were all complicating life suddenly seemed fine to me. ''I'd like that, but let me check with my mother. Hold on a second.''

My mother was still sitting at the table, staring absentmindedly at the roses. ''It's David, a friend from school. He wants me to go to the movies in an hour. Is that okay?''

''Cath, you mean you'd leave me to sort this all out by myself?''

''Yes.''

She laughed. ''Fine, then, you just go. I hope you feel guilty.''

''I won't,'' I replied, laughing too. Back to the phone I went. ''It's okay, David.'' We hung up after brief directions on how to find our apartment. I went back to my mother.

''Who is this David?'' she asked, resuming her mother role.

''You already said yes, so it's too late to ask that now. But since you must know, he's a hardened criminal just out of the county jail, and he drives a hearse.''

''Cath!''

''Kidding, Mom. Just kidding. He's a friend of Mary's and Mark's, and he works at the grocery store, and he got the night off unexpectedly and decided to ask me to a movie. And just remember that all of this is much less complicated than the mess you've gotten yourself into. Besides, now you'll have some privacy to resolve things with Mr. Donelly. That poor man. How must it feel to be in love with such a temptress that ex-husbands come back from afar to woo her?''

"Cath, you just stop right there. You know that's not true. Why don't you go get ready for your date? Suddenly I'm delighted you're going out!"

"Good—my plan worked." I dashed to my room before she could throw something at me, probably the roses, vase and all.

I know that according to those etiquette books, boys are supposed to ask girls out days in advance to show that they respect them or something. Actually, it was much better that David had asked me out with only an hour's notice, because that way I hardly had any time to get nervous about it the way I did the first time I went out with Tony. That was a nightmare—two days of being a basket case. This way, by the time I had showered, dried my hair, fixed my face, and gotten dressed, the doorbell was ringing. I could hear Mom answer it, and I heard David making polite conversation. After one more swipe of the brush through my hair, I went out to join them. Mr. Donelly was still nowhere in sight. "David!" I said pleasantly. "Are you ready to go?" I grabbed my jacket out of the closet. David looked relieved. "Have a nice evening without me," I said sweetly to my mother. She glared, but what could she say?

It was kind of weird. David and I drove to the mall, and at my request we walked down the mall and bought cookies before we went to the end where the movie theaters were. Then we went to see a new adventure movie with this handsome Australian man as the lead. I know that doesn't sound weird at all, but it was—because that's almost exactly what Tony and I did on our first date. The movie was different, but the rest was the same.

No, that is not true. The whole date was different. I was calm with David. We chatted about school, sports, movies, normal kinds of things. During the movie, when he took my hand, it was no big deal. If he held my hand, that was fine; if he hadn't, that would have been fine too. After the movie, he took me straight home because his father was working second shift and needed the car by 11:00. That was fine, too. The only awkward moment came at my door. It was almost eleven, so I knew that I didn't need to invite him in. We had said good night and all the normal "I had a good time" and "I did, too" things. Then he just stood there. I knew that he was having a difficult time deciding whether or not to kiss me, so I kissed him, just a quick kiss on the lips. Then I opened the door and went in.

It wasn't anything at all like that with Tony. When he touched my hand, I lost complete interest in the movie screen. When he kissed me, I felt like doors were being opened into new universes. With David, everything was just—fine.

I looked for my mother and Mr. Donelly, but they weren't in the kitchen or living room and the bedroom door was shut with no light showing.

The roses were gone from the dining room table.

Chapter Seventeen

The rest of the weekend passed uneventfully. Mom just smiled sweetly when I asked her if Mr. Donelly had gotten over his jealousy. He had stopped twitching, so I guessed the answer was yes. Actually, he fixed us a wonderful dinner on Sunday—filet mignon with mushrooms, asparagus, baked potatoes, and chocolate mousse for dessert. As I told Mom, the man was definitely growing on me.

Monday morning, I went looking for Bulldozer Boy. I had a good reason—I still had his books from Friday. It took some doing—first I had to go to the office to find out what homeroom he was in, and then I had to find the room, only to find no Bulldozer Boy. I asked the teacher if Robert Sullivan was in her homeroom and she said yes, but that he never arrived until just as the bell rang.

I couldn't decide what to do. If I waited for Bulldozer Boy, I'd be late for homeroom; if I tried to find him after homeroom, he'd be whizzing to his first-period class. I didn't think I was quick enough to hand off the pile of books to someone moving that fast. Finally I asked the teacher which seat was Robert's. She pointed to the one in the far back corner. I shouldn't even have had to ask. I put the books on the desk, hoping that he'd be in homeroom later to get them.

Next I went to look for Mary. She was leaning on the wall outside of her homeroom, engrossed in conversation with Mark. I didn't know if that made me happy or mad. As I walked by, unnoticed, they kissed. I fought down the urge to order Mary not to dare leave for french fries.

I didn't see David until before seventh period. He, Mark, Tony, and several others were leaning against the Junior Wall when I got there. Right after I stopped, Bulldozer Boy blew by. Mark started to laugh.

"Well, he's stopped bleeding—for now," Mark remarked.

I looked at him searchingly. "What's that supposed to mean?"

"Never mind, Cath. It's none of your concern." Mark turned back to Tony and began talking about cars.

I was infuriated by Mark's attitude, but before I could say anything more, David moved next to me. "I really enjoyed our date Friday night," he said.

"Thanks for suggesting it." As far as I could see, nothing had happened that was especially enjoyable, but it was nice of him to say that.

"We'll have to go out again some night soon. I'm not sure when I have to work next weekend, but I'll let you know as soon as the schedule's posted. Hopefully this time I'll be able to give you a little more notice."

"Fine," I said. That's exactly what it was, too. I wasn't thrilled or excited or flattered or weak-kneed. David was being nice, and I appreciated that. After all, not that many boys paid any attention at all to me, let alone asked me out. It wasn't that I didn't want to go out with David, and there was no reason at all not to like him.

"I'll talk to you soon," I said, and started off for

class. I turned back around to say goodbye to Mark and suddenly lost my ability to speak. Tony was staring at me with a strange expression on his face. Had he overheard my conversation with David? He was close enough to, but I had assumed he was talking to Mark and not paying any attention to David or me. Maybe I'd been wrong. Suddenly I felt guilty.

I walked into Spanish class confused and angry. Why did I feel guilty? I hadn't done anything wrong. Tony and I weren't dating, so I certainly could go out with anyone I wanted to. After that phone call back when Bulldozer Boy had decked me, I'd hoped that Tony would ask me out, but he hadn't. Besides, he was undoubtedly going out with half of the junior class and a quarter of the senior class. Why should I feel guilty?

I barely had time to sit down before Mr. Anderson sent me back to Bulldozer Boy to review for the next day's test. I had forgotten all about him. I threw my books down on the desk next to his, then turned to look at him. There was a large Band-Aid above his eye, and the area seemed to have swelled into a considerable lump. At least there was no blood dripping. I looked down on his desk, and sure enough, his books were piled there. Bulldozer Boy looked at the books, then looked at me and gave about a quarter of a smile. I guessed that was as much of a thank you as I was going to get. He started writing a list of the vocabulary that we were responsible for on the test.

After school I found Mary and offered her a ride home. She seemed a little less tense than usual, which was a relief.

"Mary, did Mark hit Bulldozer Boy?"

She looked at me in surprise. "What a strange thing to ask. Why would my sweet Mark do a thing like that?"

Her sweet Mark. Obviously she had stopped hating all males, or at least one in particular. "It was just something he said."

"What did he say?"

I told her about his comment that Bulldozer Boy had stopped bleeding—for now.

"I don't know, Cath. But if he did hit him, it's your fault."

"*My* fault? How do you figure it's my fault?"

"Well, you know how mad Mark was that Bulldozer Boy ran you down the first day of school. If he did do something to him, it's because of that."

Great, I thought. That had to be the stupidest thing I ever heard. I quickly changed the subject.

I had barely gotten home when the phone rang. It was my mother.

"Cath, I need a big favor."

I knew I'd have to say yes. My mother hardly ever asked me for favors. She ordered or she asked in such a way that I could not say no; this wasn't like her. "What is it?"

"I want you to join me and your father for dinner at Scotty's at 6:00."

Scotty's was, without a doubt, my favorite restaurant. It was small and cozy, and the menu changed every day. My mother knew Scotty himself because of some legal problem she'd helped him with, and he always treated us like visiting royalty.

"You know I love Scotty's, but what does Dad want?"

"I don't know, and that's why I want you there."

"Mom, aren't you a little old to need a chaperone?"

"Cath, that's not the case at all. I'd just feel more comfortable if you were there."

"Will Mr. Donelly be there?"

"No. Your father specifically asked that he not be included."

"And I bet Mr. Donelly would feel more comfortable if I were there. Mom, I don't think it's fair to put me in the middle of all this."

"I know, Cath, and I feel bad about it. But look at it this way—whatever your father and I discuss will ultimately have to do with you, because that's how our lives connect now. Wouldn't you rather be there to give your point of view rather than having us talk about you behind your back?"

"I'll meet you at your office a few minutes before six. We can walk there together."

"Thanks, Cath. It will be all right." Somehow she didn't sound convinced.

The whole conversation did not put me in an especially good mood. It sounded like my father had deliberately set out to have dinner alone with Mom, and he sure wouldn't be thrilled to see me there. I, on the other hand, was not thrilled at being where I wasn't wanted.

I tried to discipline myself to do some homework, but my mind refused to cooperate. Instead of focusing on Spanish vocabulary or the short story I had to read for English, it kept mixing together David, Tony, Mark, Mary, Bulldozer Boy, my father, my mother, and Mr. Donelly. Finally I gave up. Even the Ludlum book couldn't hold my attention, so I simply stared into space for a while. It was a relief when I saw that it was almost time to leave to meet Mom. I changed into a pair of wool pants and a pale blue sweater that she had bought me, and left. I wasn't sure that the coming hours would be pleasant, but at least I would know *something* at the end. I was getting tired of a life with no answers.

I don't know who was more nervous as we walked

to Scotty's, Mom or me. We were on time, but Dad was already there when we walked down the steps to the restaurant's entrance below street level. As we approached Dad's table, I was behind Mom, and he must not have seen me at first.

Dad jumped to his feet and held out his hand. "Angela! You look lovely tonight." Then he saw me and his smile dimmed. "Cath, I didn't realize you were joining us." There was a noticeable lack of enthusiasm in his voice.

"I asked her to," my mother said quickly. She looked at me, her eyes giving a silent apology.

"How nice," my father said. "It's just that we have some matters to discuss that I felt could best be handled by the two of us."

"Anything we have to discuss involves Cath, and she's old enough to have a say in it," my mother said firmly.

In a way, I was angry. My father could have at least pretended to be a little less disappointed. In another way, though, I thought maybe my mother was right. I'd rather get this father issue settled once and for all.

Scotty came over personally to greet us and to recommend some specials of the day. "Will John be joining you also?" he asked innocently. Mom and Mr. Donelly ate there frequently, and Scotty loved to discuss cooking hints with Mr. Donelly.

"No, he won't," my father said abruptly.

Scotty realized his mistake, mouthed a secretive "sorry" to my mother, and left. What a happy trio we were.

The waitress took our orders, and I tried to calm myself by listening to the music playing in the background. I figured that maybe this discussion would wait until after we'd eaten, and I wasn't in the mood to help Mom with small talk. She, however, jumped right in.

"William, what is it you wanted to discuss?"

I guess she's the one I inherit my impatience from.

"Angela, this can wait." My father looked significantly at me. I felt like getting up and walking out, but I'd ordered fettucini alfredo and I wanted to at least taste it.

"There's no need to wait. Please—go right ahead." Dad might as well get it over with, since it was obvious that Mom was in one of her forceful moods.

Dad sighed, then angled his chair toward her, almost turning his back on me. I studied the rose on our table as if it were a fascinating new species.

"Angela, I've been doing a lot of thinking, both before I left Saudi Arabia and after. I think I've been unfair to you."

He paused, and after waiting thirty seconds or so, my mother said, "Unfair in what way, William?"

"I think I panicked too quickly when you started to become interested in leading a more independent life. I interpreted every step you took out of the house as a step away from me."

"That wasn't what I intended," said Mom. "I simply was stagnating being a housewife, and I needed more." She looked at me and quickly continued. "I loved staying home and taking care of Cath, but as she grew older and more independent, I needed more to fill my life. Otherwise I would have smothered her, and bored you to tears."

"You've never been boring, Angela."

"Well, that's nice to hear, but I can't imagine that it's very interesting to hear about my day when the most exciting thing I did was comparison shop for avocados."

I almost laughed, but my concentration on the rose rescued me. My mother doesn't even like avocados.

My father continued, even though my mother wasn't making it easy for him. "Actually I'm quite proud of all you've accomplished since I've been gone, law school, a career—it's quite impressive."

"Thank you, William. It's very important to me, and all the more so because I did it by myself."

There, I thought. Mom sure was holding a tough line.

Dad seemed to be squirming a little, and beads of perspiration appeared on his forehead. "Once I was back and saw you again, I realized that I haven't met a woman who compares to you. I've realized that perhaps I can now accept a woman who doesn't fit the conventional mold of wife and mother."

Now it was my mother's turn to squirm. I had a feeling that suddenly she wasn't so glad that she had made me come along. I could feel her turn toward me, but I refused to lift my eyes from the rose.

"William, what are you saying?" My mother's voice was soft yet determined.

"What I wanted to say to you tonight is that I think we should make another try at our relationship. Perhaps what we once had could be reborn in a new and even better way. Then maybe the three of us can be a family again."

I gulped. I'm not sure what I had expected of this evening, but it wasn't this.

"William, I . . ." My mother was obviously struggling to find words.

"Please, Angela, I don't expect an answer now. Just think about it. We'll talk again when you've had time to consider what I've said."

I sat quietly for minute after minute. The conversation shifted to the painting on the wall next to our table. To myself I kept repeating, Don't do it, don't do it, don't do it, but I couldn't help myself.

"Dad, why did you start insisting that I come live with you? And why are you trying to take over my mother's life now?"

I don't know who was more surprised by my interruption, my mother or my father. Both wheeled around to look at me as if I had suddenly sprouted in the chair.

"What do you mean?" my father said.

"Exactly what I asked," I said coldly, trying to shove down the anger that had started to burn upward from my stomach to my mouth.

"I was just concerned about what was best for you," my father said.

"Sorry, but I find that hard to believe." My voice came out more loudly than I meant it to.

"Cath," my mother began, but then she stopped. I think she knew I needed to get this out in the open.

"Dad, you can't just pretend the last four years never happened. Mom and I have both built lives without you."

"I am your father no matter where I am," he retaliated.

"Yes, you are, but that doesn't give you the right to come barging back into our lives and try to take them over. You're not spending any time at all thinking about what I want, or what Mom wants. All you know is what you want. It's just so selfish."

"Is it so bad to want to reunite our family?"

"It's just not that easy," I said, my voice softening at the sight of the pain in his eyes. "I need time to get used to having a father again."

"And I need time to get used to having an ex-husband in town," my mother added softly.

"What about me?" my father asked. "What about

my needs? I want to be a father again, a husband again. I've missed that.''

"It's just not that easy," I repeated.

Suddenly I couldn't stand it any more. I had to get out of there. "Mom, I need to leave." My voice was quivering, even though I didn't want it to.

"I'll go with you," she said, starting to get out of her chair.

"Please stay," I said. "I really need some time alone. I'm not ready to talk about this, so there's nothing to be gained by your leaving." I managed to regain control of my voice.

"You sure you're okay to drive?" Mom said, giving in, knowing me well enough to realize that I meant what I said.

"I'm sure." I turned to my father. "Enjoy your dinner."

I left just as the waitress was bringing the food.

Chapter Eighteen

I drove home in a fog of anger and hurt and sadness. I had been scared when my father had started his demands that I live with him, and I had resented the fact that he thought my mother was harming me in some way by having Mr. Donelly live with us. Still, though, I had been just a little bit flattered. After all, it had seemed that my father really did love me so much that he wanted me with him and was concerned about my welfare. Now I felt tricked. For the first time, I wished my father were back in Saudi Arabia, out of my life. He was complicating everything. So much for my fantasies of how wonderful it would be to have a father nearby. So far, I hated it. My mother and I weren't objects to be thrown away and then picked up again at will.

I slammed into the apartment and paced around. I couldn't sit still, couldn't find any kind of resolution that would put my mind at peace. Mr. Donelly wasn't home, and I wondered briefly where my mother had exiled him to for the evening.

I considered calling Mary. I just couldn't do it, though; she had enough problems of her own without hearing about mine. Suddenly I knew exactly who I wanted to talk to. Before I could think about it and stop myself from doing it, I went to the phone and dialed a familiar number.

On the third ring, I heard the voice I wanted to hear. "Hello?"

"Tony, it's Cath. I just wanted to tell you that I understand something now that I never understood before, even when you tried to explain it to me."

"What's that, Catherine?"

"What it feels like to hate your father." Somehow it felt good to say those words. I knew that Tony was the only one who would understand—Tony, who called his father the Ogre and who never had anything good to say about him.

"Catherine, you know you don't hate your father. That's a harsh thing to say."

"Why? You say it all the time."

"That's different. Your family has always been really important to you. Mine has always been nothing to me."

Actually, that wasn't really true. Tony's family had been a source of pain and bitterness for him. His parents had told him that he had been an accident, and not an especially happy one at that.

"It's not all that different, Tony."

"Catherine, you're obviously upset. Are you at home? Do you want me to come over?"

I did, more than anything else in the world. The only problem was that Mom would probably be home before very long, and she wasn't especially fond of Tony anymore, especially after all the problems he had caused me last year. I wasn't in the mood for any more family disturbances.

"Could we meet somewhere?"

There was a pause before Tony spoke. "Oh, I see. I'm not exactly welcome in the Berry house these days."

"Tony, please." Tears started to spill down my face. My anger was starting to die down, and now I felt terribly sad. I felt rejected enough; I couldn't deal with making Tony feel rejected too. "I'm sorry. It was a bad idea to call you. I'll see you in school tomorrow."

"No you don't, Catherine. I'll meet you at McDonalds in ten minutes. Okay?"

I didn't say anything for a moment. What was I doing?

"Ten minutes, Catherine. Promise you'll be there. If you're not, I'll be at your house."

"I'll be there. Thanks." The phone went dead as he hung up.

I stared at the refrigerator, the place where I always left messages for my mother. I knew she'd be worried if I wasn't home when she got back, but she would be more worried if she knew I was with Tony. I considered lying—that I was at Mary's, or at the library—but I was afraid that my mother would come after me. Finally I left the refrigerator naked. After all, I only wanted to talk to Tony for a few minutes, and I'd probably be home before her.

The VW was still warm, and I tried to shut off my mind as I drove the familiar roads to McDonalds. I knew that if I had thought much before calling Tony I would have realized it would be a mistake, but it was too late for second thoughts. Besides, he would understand.

After I pulled in the lot, I wasn't sure what to do next. I didn't see Tony's motorcycle or his father's car. Of course, he could have parked on the other side, or he could be waiting inside. As I tried to figure out what to do next, someone tapped on the passenger's side window. I jumped so much that my head hit the ceiling of the car. I smiled when I saw Tony's face, and I unfastened my seatbelt and reached across to unlock the door.

"Do you want to go inside and get something to eat?" he asked, opening the door and sticking his head in.

The thought of food made me slightly sick. "I don't want anything, but if you're hungry . . ."

Tony got into the car, shutting the door firmly behind him. Suddenly I didn't know what to say. Maybe this had been a serious mistake.

"Talk to me, Catherine." Tony's voice was gentle, and that was all it took. Tears started streaming down my face. I felt like a fool, but I just couldn't help it.

"Come here." Tony reached for me, and his arms were around me, and I was crying full force, face buried in the comfort of his shoulder. Tony didn't say anything, just rubbed my back and held me tight. Finally I grew quiet, all cried out. I didn't want to lift my face. I didn't want to think what my face must look like. Blindly I searched my pocket for a tissue and self-consciously blew my nose, then burrowed my head in Tony's shoulder again. He let me rest for a while, then took my face in both of his hands and lifted my chin until I was looking up at him.

"Now talk to me, Catherine."

I did. I told him the whole story about my father, at first hesitantly, then with increasing speed and determination. Telling it seemed to give my anger a new birth, although my anger was muted by sadness and a certain exhaustion.

"You don't hate him, Catherine," Tony finally said.

"How do you know?" I asked.

"If you hated him, you wouldn't be angry. You'd just be cold inside."

"Is that the way you feel about your father?"

"Yes. But that's me, not you."

"Why? Aren't I allowed to hate just like you?"

"No," Tony replied.

"Why not?" I challenged.

"Because you're different from me, very different."

"That doesn't mean I can't hate."

"Yes it does, Catherine. That's exactly what it means. And that's what makes you a better person than me."

"I'm not better," I answered.

"Yes you are," Tony said quietly. "Do you hate me?"

"No," I answered. Tony had caused me more pain than anyone else in my life, but I had never hated him.

"You deserve to," Tony said. "I made you take responsibility for my mistakes, and that was wrong."

That was the first time Tony had ever admitted that. He had been driving my car and had been stopped by a policeman. Since he had been drinking, he convinced me to switch seats with him. I had, and that had been the end of the relationship. I don't mean to make it sound that simple; it wasn't. There were lots of other things that had led up to that night, problems with Tony's attitude toward life and love and the future, but that had been the final action that made me break up with him.

"Tony, I never hated you. I was afraid of you, afraid of what was happening to my life because of you."

"If you can't hate me, you can't hate your father." He paused. "Why aren't you afraid of me now?"

That was a question for which I could find no easy answer. My silence must have been an answer, of sorts.

"Are you still afraid, Catherine?"

"Yes." The answer was out before I had time to think about it.

"Why?"

I burrowed my head in his shoulder again, knowing

that I would have to answer but not wanting to meet his eyes as I did.

"I'm afraid of how much you can make me feel."

"Is it bad to feel?" he asked.

"No, but you can also make me feel great pain, and I'm afraid of that."

"I never meant to hurt you."

"I believe you, Tony. It's just that you did, or at least I let you hurt me, and I really believed that we were both better off without each other."

"And now?"

"Now I just needed to talk to someone who would understand what I was feeling, and you were the one I thought of."

"Is that all?"

No, it wasn't all. What I had wanted even more than someone who understood was someone who would hold me in his arms and make me feel safe, even if just for a little while. And the person I had wanted to hold me was Tony.

"Yes." That wasn't a completely honest answer, but it was the best I could do.

"You didn't want to talk to David?"

I looked at him, startled. Then it hit me. Tony *had* overheard that conversation at the Junior Wall. I answered honestly.

"No, I didn't want to talk to David."

"I'm glad." With that, Tony once again tilted my head up to his, and this time he kissed me. It was a wonderful kiss, and it was Tony who ended it, not me. I could taste beer on his breath, but somehow it didn't matter.

He reached out and touched my hair, stroking it, gently pushing it back. It was a gesture I remembered well. "Take care, Pretty Girl. Call me if you need me." With that, he was out of the car and gone.

I slumped back in the seat, breathless. Pretty Girl? He had never called me that before. He had always called me Catherine instead of Cath, and he had once called me a bitch, but never Pretty Girl. How wonderful it sounded coming from him.

I drove home slowly, savoring the moment, not wanting to go back into the reality of home and my mother and all of those problems. I was relieved to find the apartment dark, and I went to my room, undressed, and crawled into bed. It was still early, but I simply wanted to retreat. I didn't want to think, but I knew I'd have to.

About an hour later, I heard my mother come in. I heard other footsteps behind her, and I recognized them as Mr. Donelly's. Mom came directly to my room.

"Cath, are you all right?"

"I suppose." I certainly had calmed down, but I didn't want to tell her that Tony deserved the credit for that.

"You need to know what your father . . ."

I interrupted. "Mom, can this wait until tomorrow? I'm really not ready to talk yet."

She looked a little surprised. "Are you sure you want to wait?"

"Positive," I said.

Mom didn't look happy, but she respected my need for time. That's one of the things I've always appreciated about her. "Tomorrow?" she asked.

"Tomorrow," I promised.

Mom left, closing my door behind her. I didn't envy her. If I was confused, think how she must feel. Besides, she had to explain all of this to Mr. Donelly.

I curled under the covers, trying to recapture the security I'd felt in Tony's arms.

Chapter Nineteen

Imagine my surprise the next morning when I walked into the kitchen and saw my mother. Normally I don't see her at all in the morning since I'm up and out before she gets out of bed. She was definitely not a morning person, and she claimed that one of the reasons she loved her job as a lawyer was that she could go in at 9:30.

She was sitting at the kitchen table, a mug of coffee in her hand. She looked tired and worried, and my first thought was that she was sick.

"Mom, what are you doing up so early?" I opened the refrigerator door and took out English muffins, butter, jelly, and orange juice.

"It's surprising how easy it is when you never get to sleep."

I didn't say anything and let my mom continue.

"Cath, I feel so bad about last night. I know he loves you, but I also know he was wrong to make you feel so pressured."

"There's no 'feel' about it, Mom. That's exactly what he did, and you know it." I felt last night's anger returning.

"Yes, I'm afraid you're right. I talked to him at length after you left, and he knows now how wrong he was to do that."

"Great," I said. The bell sounded on the toaster

oven, and I retrieved my English muffin, slammed it down on a plate, and slathered butter and jelly on it.

"Cath, I know you're angry . . ."

"Aren't you?" I interrupted.

"Yes," she admitted.

"Want half of this?" I said, pointing to the muffin.

"No," she said. "What I want is to try to make you understand all of this mess."

"Good luck," I said. I didn't mean to be harsh with her, but I wasn't in the mood to be tolerant and forgiving.

"Cath, your father is a lonely man. I feel sorry for him."

"Sorry for him?" I exploded.

"Yes," she replied firmly. "He sure isn't a perfect man, as we both know, but he's a lonely man who is desperately looking for some answers."

"Well the answer isn't to demand instant love from both of us."

"I know that, and he knows that, too—now. It's just that after our divorce, he went to Saudi Arabia with the company, and he thought that he was starting a whole new life."

"And didn't he?" I slapped two pieces of bread down on the counter, then started making myself a cheese and pickle sandwich for lunch.

"Yes and no," Mom replied. "He certainly did well enough professionally. He moved up to the head of the engineering department at his site."

"Good for him," I said sarcastically.

"Personally, however, he never found much of a life," Mom continued. "He told me last night that he dated a few different women, colleagues and such, but that he never found an enduring relationship. What he did instead was to immerse himself in his work."

"Am I supposed to feel sorry for him?" I asked

"No, but I hoped you'd start to understand," Mom replied quietly. "When he was transferred back here, he saw how grown-up you were, and realized how fast time was passing."

"Then why did he treat me like a little girl with no mind of her own?" I asked, slapping pickles on top of the cheese.

"He didn't want to admit it. You have to realize that he's never had much experience with a teenage daughter, so he treated you in the only way he knew how—like the child he used to know."

"Is this supposed to be my fault?" I opened the refrigerator door, then slammed it shut after I took out a jar of sweet and spicy mustard.

"No, Cath, none of this is your fault," Mom said. "What I think happened is that your father started to look back over his life, and in his memory the happiest time was back when you were a child and we were a family together."

"So he decided he wanted that back?" I put the top piece of bread on my sandwich, savagely cut it in half, and reached for the Saran Wrap.

"Yes," Mom replied simply.

"There are a couple of problems with that," I said as I ripped off the plastic wrap and battled it impatiently as it clung to itself. "First of all, I'm not that little child anymore, and second of all, you're divorced from him and leading your own life."

"I know," Mom said.

You know, when I think about it, it's really weird. When my parents first separated and got divorced, I prayed every night that they would get back together again. I wove fantasies in my mind where I was sick and they realized over my hospital bed that they still loved each other and then I got better and we lived happily ever after. Suddenly, now I realized that the possibility existed that my parents would get back together, and I wasn't the least bit happy. In fact, I was afraid. I mean, I felt like I knew Mr. Donelly better than I knew my father.

"Mom, you're not going to . . . you don't want to . . . are you going to . . ." I fumbled helplessly for words.

"Are your father and I going to reconcile?" My mom sounded a little like a lawyer, but it was a relief to have the thought put into words, any words.

"Are you?" I threw the wrapped sandwich into a brown bag, then brought my orange juice to the table and sat across from my mother.

"Is that what you want?" she asked.

"Don't you dare make this my decision," I snapped. "I didn't start this, and I'm not going to end it. You're the adult."

My mother smiled. "I was just checking," she said. "I'd never ask you to make that decision for me. I have to admit that as much as I love you, I would never live with a man just to please you. Even if you were happy, if I weren't, I'd find subtle little ways to take that out on you, which would be horrible."

All of this was fine, but it wasn't an answer. "What did you decide about Dad?"

"He wants me to give him a chance, to see him, spend time with him."

"You're going to date my father?" I asked in amazement.

"That's what he asked me to do," she replied.

"What did you say?"

"I told him I'd think about it."

I looked at her in amazement. "Mom, what are you going to do about Mr. Donelly? I don't see how you can live with him and date my father."

"It is rather confusing, isn't it," my mother said.

"No wonder you didn't sleep last night," I said.

"Cath, all I promised to do was think about it. It doesn't mean that I'll go out with him. I'm angry with him for the way he's treated us both, but at the same time I feel sorry for him, sorry for his loneliness."

"That's not your fault."

"I know. But he *is* your father."

"Leave me out of this," I said.

"I can't," Mom replied. "You're a part of everything."

I looked at her, saw her reddened eyes, noticed the shadows under them. I no longer felt angry. "Mom, I'll be all right no matter what."

"Will you?" she asked.

"I think so," I said. "At least I know I've got you."

"Couldn't get rid of me if you tried," Mom stated.

"Have you told Mr. Donelly about all of this?" I asked.

"Not yet," Mom said. "I wanted to have a chance to think it through before I did."

"And?" I prompted.

"And I think I'm not done thinking yet."

I shook my head, then smiled at her. "And I thought it was hard to be a teenager."

"You'll be the first to know when I get this figured out," she said.

"Thanks," I replied. "I'd better get ready for school."

I left her sitting at the table, staring into the bottom of her coffee cup as if it held the answers.

Chapter Twenty

I was in a fog as I went through that school day. My mother dating my father? This was all rather bizarre. The fog lifted abruptly at lunch, however. As usual, Mary and I met. Mary had been having a rather calm day so there was no need for an emergency talk in the library conference room. Instead, we went to our normal table in the cafeteria. The cafeteria wasn't especially crowded, so no one else shared the table even though there were four chairs around it. That was usual for us; although Mary has lots of friends, we typically eat alone, finding that a good time to talk. We ate first lunch, and Mark, Tony, David, and the rest of that group all ate second lunch, so that made it easier to keep Mary calm.

The table we sat at was about in the middle of the back wall, on the opposite side of the cafeteria from the doors. I had barely started on my cheese and pickle sandwich when I first knew that something was wrong. It's weird how you know things like that, but in a big high school like mine, you get a second sense about when something's going to happen. I think this time the clue was that the cafeteria got quieter than usual. Normally it's loud, hundreds of conversations punctuated with loud laughter and the scraping of chairs as people come and go. Suddenly, though, the noise lessened, just as if someone had turned down the volume control on the stereo. I looked at Mary; she, too, was scanning the room, looking for an explanation.

It didn't take long to find the answer. About three tables toward the center of the cafeteria from us, two boys were on their feet shouting at each other. I didn't know either of them, but they were obviously riled up. The screaming was what had originally gained the attention of others nearby, and suddenly it was as if a tidal wave of humanity rushed toward those two boys. In a matter of seconds, a ring formed around them, and their shouts were drowned out by the people screaming at the two boys to fight. Before my view was totally blocked, I could see that nobody had any interest whatsoever in stopping the two from fighting; this had become a spectator sport.

I looked around the cafeteria. It seemed like everyone in there except for Mary and me was gathered in a huge circle. There wasn't a teacher in sight. Early in the period the teachers who have lunch duty usually monitor the line at the food serving area, and they didn't stand a chance of getting through the mob. Mary and I were pinned back against the wall, our table shoved back against us by those trying to get a better view. The two boys must have actually started fighting, because I could hear screams of "Get him." I also could hear chairs crash, and a table suddenly tipped over, unbalanced by the four boys standing on it to get a better view.

The crowd surged on either side of our table, and Mary and I looked at each other mutely. We were on our feet now, the table shoved right against us, furniture crashing all around. Suddenly another fight broke out to the right of the original one; I think that one started because one guy elbowed the other in the face trying to get closer to the first fight. By this point, some girls had begun to scream, others were shouting, some were cheering as if it were a football game, and the entire cafeteria was electric with tension and excitement. Far off I could faintly hear the bellows of a couple of teachers yelling at the kids to let them through, but there wasn't a chance. There was a solid mass of bodies, and many of them didn't want the fun to end.

I was shaking, and I was as near to panic as I'd been in a long time. I wanted out of there more than I wanted anything in my life. I was trapped by people I suddenly hated. Where had this blood lust come from? Why did these people want to see two human beings bash each other's brains out? What was fun and exciting about being mobbed around a fight that only a few could actually see, caught up in something they didn't even understand? Who was fighting? Why were they fighting? These people didn't care. They just seemed to want to see blood. I hated it. I knew that I could be smashed into the wall until my guts came out of my mouth and no one would even notice.

I looked at Mary. She was pale, her lips almost blue. Her eyes were fastened on the second fight, and suddenly I realized why. Through the crowd I caught a glimpse of one of the two, and it was Mark. I hadn't recognized him earlier, but somehow Mary had. She let out a scream.

"Cath, we have to do something. It's Mark. We've got to help him."

I looked at her in amazement. We were trapped behind the table, and then there were circles of people at least twenty deep between Mark and us. Besides, what were we going to do if we actually could get to him? Did Mary want us to throw our bodies between the fighters?

"Mary, we can't. We need to get out of here."

Actually, my request was about as difficult to achieve as hers. The cafeteria doors were on the other side, and there wasn't even clearance along the back wall to get away from the crowd.

"Cath, we have to do something." Mary looked as if she was either going to get completely hysterical or pass out, and I wasn't feeling too calm myself. Several other fights had erupted as well, and the crowd shifted slightly with the action. It made me sick.

I've never considered myself claustrophobic, although I do hate elevators and I have nightmares about being shut in a prison cell and hearing the barred door clang shut. Suddenly, though, that cafeteria was a torture chamber for me. I felt like the screaming people were taking up all the oxygen, and I began to gasp for breath. The walls seemed to move, closing in on me, and the table turned into a rock barrier that could never be moved. In fact, I shoved frantically against the table, trying to create some breathing space, but my strength was powerless against the wall of bodies facing away from me.

Suddenly I began to scream. "Get out of my way. Let me out of here. Move!" I may as well have been whispering. Not even one head turned. My heart was pounding, and I could feel a cold sweat covering my skin. My hands shook as I pushed frantically against the table. Mary stood looking at me, motionless.

"Help me move this," I screamed at her. She shoved at the table with me, but we couldn't move it, didn't even have enough space to get leverage to use our legs. I briefly considered trying to get under it, but I was pinned too tightly for even that.

It seemed like hours had passed since lunch had started; it seemed like there had been enough time for the National Guard to arrive, but I guess it really was only a few minutes. Still no teachers had breached the masses; I wouldn't have blamed them for not even trying. I had an insane urge to yell "Fire" to see if that would get some attention away from the fighting, but even in the midst of my panic I knew that wouldn't be a good idea. If that scream were picked up, people would be killed smashing toward the doors.

I had no answers, but I was desperate to find some soon. Then I saw a break. It was hard to notice at first, but to my right, near the back wall, someone was clearing a way through the mob. The bodies barely separated, and the gap closed again immediately. I assumed that it was an administrator, someone powerful. Then the crowd split briefly nearer to me, and I knew exactly who it was. I caught a glimpse of a brown corduroy jacket, and I recognized the barreling movement. Bulldozer Boy. Even this mob knew to clear the way for him.

He was coming closer and closer, and I grabbed Mary's hand, ready to yank her after me if I had the chance. I screamed, "Robert," screamed louder than I've ever screamed before, but even so I don't think he could have heard me. Still, though, he headed directly for me. Soon he barged through the last few people and was at the edge of our table.

"Get me out of here," I said, and it wasn't a scream but almost a whisper. Bulldozer Boy grabbed the edge of the table and savagely yanked it forward, and suddenly Mary and I had a couple of inches of freedom. It was enough. I sidled sideways, dragging Mary after me. Once we were free of the table, I lined myself up right behind Bulldozer Boy. He glanced back, nodded slightly, and then we were off. At first we moved pretty slowly, Mary and I ducking through the holes that he created before they could close again. Then he gained some momentum, and we had to practically run to keep up with him, tripping over feet, banging against chairs but moving, always moving. Eventually we were at the corner, and at that point the crowd thinned. We followed Bulldozer Boy down the adjoining wall and finally were at the front corner where there was a door. As we rushed out, about five or six teachers were rushing in.

The hallway was an oasis of tranquillity compared to the cafeteria. I followed Bulldozer Boy down to the end of that first hallway, and then my legs gave out. I was shaking so badly that I couldn't run anymore, and I abruptly stopped, causing Mary to plow into me. We looked at each other wordlessly, and then we both leaned against the wall, panting. The air was about ten degrees cooler, and the silence was almost a physical presence. The screams of the cafeteria were only faint echoes.

Tears started to stream down my face. I hated high school and the people in it. I wanted out.

"Mary, let's leave," I said. "My car's in the parking lot. Let's get out of this place."

"I can't," she said. "I have to find out what happened to Mark."

"Who cares," I said harshly. "I don't want any part of this whole place."

"I care," said Mary. Suddenly I realized how thoughtless my statement had been. Mark had been her boyfriend for a long time now; of course she cared. It all struck me as stupid and sad and terrible—the boy who just might be a father was getting into a fight in the cafeteria and might be hurt and would undoubtedly be suspended. How mature.

Meanwhile, my thoughts would be of no comfort to Mary. "Well, we're sure not going back in there," I said. "Eventually he's bound to end up at the nurse's office. Let's wait there."

Mary agreed, and we headed further down the next

hallway and then the next. Suddenly I stopped, horrified.

"Bulldozer Boy!" I gasped, covering my mouth with my hands.

"What about him?" Mary asked.

I looked around frantically, but of course he was nowhere in sight. "He just rescued us, and we didn't even thank him. That's terrible."

"Do you really think he came to rescue us?" Mary asked.

"I don't know, but he sure headed straight for us, and whether he meant to or not, he's responsible for getting us out. That at least deserves a thank you, Mary."

"You're right," she said. "Where do you think he is?" Meanwhile she had started walking again, headed for the nurse's office.

"You wait for Mark; I'm going to look for Bulldozer Boy," I said. Mary didn't look too pleased, but she couldn't stop me.

I searched the hallways of this first floor, skirting the vicinity of the cafeteria, then started on the second floor. I never saw him, and I had no idea where else to look. I knew it was time for the bell to ring, and I headed toward my class, more from habit than anything. At least I would see him in Spanish seventh period.

He certainly deserved my thanks.

Chapter Twenty-one

Bulldozer Boy wasn't in Spanish class that day. I had no theories as to why he wasn't. He certainly had been fine at lunch when he had rescued Mary and me; in fact, he had been very fine. The more I thought about what had happened, the more I wondered how he had known I was there, and how he had known I needed help. I'd never seen him in the cafeteria before, not once. Maybe it had been an accident. Maybe he had come into the cafeteria to see what was going on and had just happened to come back to where we were. No matter what the reason, I wanted to thank him. I still shook every time I thought of the fighting, being trapped behind the table, that horrible feeling of being imprisoned by people I hated.

I had rushed to find Mary before seventh period, going to wait for her outside of her English class. She looked shaken. Mark had finally shown up at the nurse's office, escorted by a decidedly angry assistant principal. Mary said that Mark had a cut under one eye and a split lip, but otherwise he had reassured her that he was fine. This, of course, was after she almost passed out at the sight of his blood. According to the assistant principal, who had ordered Mary back to class, Mark would definitely be suspended for three days. All I could do was reassure Mary that at least he wasn't seriously injured.

It was after school that the first bright spot appeared in my day. When I left Spanish with the final bell, Tony caught up with me at my locker. I was in a fog, and at first I didn't even know that he was there. Then I felt a hand touch my hair. Startled, I jumped and gasped, then whirled around.

"Sorry," said Tony. "I didn't mean to scare you."

My heart continued pounding, but now it was for a reason other than fear. Tony looked wonderful. His dark eyes met mine, and he leaned against the locker next to mine, angling his body toward me. I turned toward my locker, shoving books in, forgetting what books I needed for homework, suddenly not caring, trying to regain my composure. Then I shut the locker door, still not looking at Tony.

"Catherine, what's wrong?" His voice was gentle, concerned. "Is it still your father?"

Considering the excitement of the day, I hadn't even given my father a thought. "No," I answered. I told him about the fight.

"I heard stories all afternoon," Tony said. "I didn't know Mark was one of them. I knew he wasn't at second lunch when I went to see if he wanted to cut out for McDonalds, but I didn't know why."

"Why was Mark even in the cafeteria during first lunch?" I asked.

"I don't know," Tony responded, "but he had to have been cutting class. He's been acting weird lately."

Great. That would reassure Mary.

"Are you sure you're okay?" he asked me. "I'm sorry I wasn't there to help."

I almost answered that Bulldozer Boy had rescued me, but I didn't. I'm not sure why. "I'm fine," I said. "Thanks for your concern."

Still Tony stood there, and I began to feel awkward.

Did he want a ride home? The buses had obviously left by now. Did he just want to stand and chat? I felt like one of us needed to make a move.

"My car's in the parking lot. Want a ride home?"

"No, but thanks anyway. I rode my motorcycle today." Tony was still looking at me. "I just wanted a chance to see you for a minute."

I smiled. Tony still knew how to make me feel special.

"Will you be around this weekend?" he asked.

That really made my heart start to pound again. "Probably," I said.

"I'll give you a call," Tony said. "Maybe we can go out or something."

"Fine," I said. I wanted to say "When? Where? Give me a plan and a time," but I didn't say anything other than "fine."

"Goodbye, Pretty Girl," Tony said. I watched as he walked away. I felt like whooping with joy. Somehow I had managed to forget all of the pain Tony had caused; all I could feel was how happy he could make me, how flattered I was that after everything, he wanted to take *me* out. I didn't know how to tell my mother, but I'd find a way.

I practically floated out of school, and I sang along with the radio the whole way home.

As soon as I got in, I washed my hair. After all, I might not have a lot of notice, and I wanted to be ready. Maybe Tony would call that very night. Friday night. We could go to the movies, then get something to eat, have a chance to talk . . . it would be great. I felt buoyant, energetic, ready to have a good time.

After my hair was dry, I began a closet search. What would I wear? Of course it was difficult to decide since I didn't know what Tony had in mind to do. Maybe he'd wait until tomorrow and then we could go to the park or take a long walk or drive down to the beach. Finally I threw myself down on the bed, fantasizing about all the possibilities.

It was almost five when the phone rang. I knew it was Tony. I raced into the kitchen, then let it ring another time so that I wouldn't look over-anxious. I was so sure it was Tony that I almost added his name to my hello.

It was my mother. What a letdown. She said that she and Mr. Donelly were going out to dinner straight from work, and that they wouldn't be home until later. I supposed that they were going to have a talk about the situation with my father. Suddenly the advantage of this struck me.

"That's great, Mom. Enjoy dinner. I may meet some kids from school tonight for a movie or something. I'll leave you a note if I do."

Mom was so preoccupied she never even commented beyond saying "Fine, Cath." She should have known that meeting "kids from school" wasn't exactly like me. I hung up quickly before she did any more thinking. This was perfect. Now all Tony had to do was call. I hadn't exactly lied to Mom, not really. Just take away the plural and it was true.

I went back to my room, happier than before. The first hour, I continued my fantasies, planning the perfect evening with Tony. I even checked the movie listings and picked the one I wanted to see, in case Tony left the decision to me. I didn't bother to fix dinner; I could have popcorn at the movies.

The second hour, I began to get a little anxious. It was still early, but if we were going to make a movie, we needed to get organized. I considered calling Tony, weighing the pros and cons. I decided it would look pushy; after all, he had said he would call me. Besides, I couldn't exactly say, look Tony, I lied to my mother so she can't give me any grief about seeing you. Let's take advantage of that. No, I'd have to wait.

By the third hour, I was getting crazy. I paced around the apartment trying to send mental messages to Tony: Call, call, call. Call now. Fifteen times I must have picked up the phone, listening for the dial tone to make sure it was working. It was eight o'clock by the time the phone finally did ring, and by then my nerves were shot from the waiting. I snatched up the phone, having reached the kitchen in two large bounds. Mentally I was calculating that we could still make a 9:15 movie, and that I needed to get out of the house before Mom and Mr. Donelly got back.

"Hi," I said, welcoming Tony's call.

Only it wasn't Tony. "Hello. This is David."

I wanted to scream. I wanted to say, how dare you call me? You're supposed to be Tony.

"Hello, David," I said with a noticeable lack of enthusiasm.

"I'm sorry to wait so long to call you, but I'm at work and this is the first break I've had," David said apologetically.

"That's okay," I said.

"I was wondering if you'd like to do something tomorrow. I have the whole day off, so we could either do something in the afternoon, or go to a movie in the evening."

He waited for a reaction. My mind was racing. How could I go out with David? Tony was going to call. What if I missed Tony's call because I was out with David? I couldn't stand the thought, but I didn't want to explain that to David.

"I'm afraid I can't make plans for tomorrow. I think I have to help my mother."

As soon as the words were out, I wanted to stuff them back in my mouth. That was a lame excuse. Why had I added that about my mother? Who would believe that?

"All day?" asked David.

"I'm not sure, and she's not home now so I can't check with her. I think we may have to go visit relatives."

"Oh," said David, and either I was getting paranoid or there was definite skepticism in his voice. "Would you like me to check back with you tomorrow?"

"Sure," I said. "That would be great." There. Now I'd done it. At least I'd have some time to think up better lies.

"I need to get back to work. I'll call you tomorrow."

I said goodbye and stomped back to my room. I was angry, and at first I thought I was angry at David. How dare he make me lie? Then I realized that wasn't fair. He was just being nice. It was right about then that the utter stupidity of what I'd said hit me. When Tony did call, we'd probably end up at the park or the mall or the movies or somewhere else where we'd be likely to run into kids from school. What if we saw David? He'd know I'd lied to him, and I'd feel like a fool. Even if I didn't see David, those guys were together every day at the Junior Wall, and someone was bound to say something about Tony and me.

I felt like a jerk. Why hadn't I been honest? Why hadn't I told him I just didn't want to go out with him? Or why hadn't I been almost honest and told him I had other plans? I did have plans with Tony—sort of.

I felt like a jerk, but I was still glad that I'd said no to David. Yes, I'd feel bad if I went out with Tony and ran into David, but there was a much worse possibility—what if I went out with David and ran into Tony? Now *that* was a nightmare possibility. David was a nice guy, but he sure wasn't Tony.

My mind raced. I felt like a hamster inside a wheel, running and running but getting nowhere.

By nine o'clock, I knew that Tony wasn't going to call. I lectured myself not to worry, that he would call tomorrow and that was better because we had a whole day to make plans for. I picked up the Ludlum book and I actually thought I was reading until I realized that I had turned ten pages and had absolutely no idea what was going on. Finally I got undressed and crawled under the covers, willing sleep to come. It must have, because I never heard Mom and Mr. Donelly come in.

Chapter Twenty-two

Saturday morning I awoke to the sounds of my mother thrashing around the apartment. She is not a morning person, and until she's awake and full of coffee, I usually try to avoid her. Suddenly, though, all of last night's tension came back to me. Tony. He hadn't called. Would he call today? In case he did, I'd better be up and in position to answer the phone before Mom did. I didn't think she'd exactly forbid me to see Tony, but I couldn't be sure. I didn't want to risk it.

I bounded out of bed, threw on a robe, and went out toward the kitchen. Mom was in the living room, dusting cloth in hand, standing on one foot and rubbing the shin of the other leg with her hand.

"Good morning, Cath. I hope I didn't wake you. I was trying to get some cleaning done before I left, but I keep running into the furniture."

That was my Mom. I had to laugh. "Mom, why don't you let me do that?" Now for the interesting part. "Where are you going?"

"John and I have some work to finish at the office. It's a big case, and we're behind schedule on it. Then we're going to drive into Philadelphia to see his Aunt Isabelle, and with any luck we'll get tickets for whatever's playing at the Shubert Theater. Want to come with us?"

"No," I answered quickly, then more calmly, "No, thanks for asking, but I think I'll stay here."

"Any particular reason?" Mom asked.

Uh oh, she was more aware today than yesterday. She knew how much I loved Philadelphia. "School work, stuff like that. I'm just sort of tired. I'd like to take it easy."

Mom looked at me searchingly, but she didn't challenge me any further. I hid my glee. This would make it easy to see Tony.

"Think you could go to the grocery store for me? I've left a list on the refrigerator."

"Sure, no problem. And I'll finish the cleaning for you." I'd better watch out or she would get suspicious. How was I going to go to the store and make sure I didn't miss Tony's call? I'd figure that out later.

"Cath, can we talk seriously for a minute?"

She'd seen through me. I'd have to tell her the truth. I'd tell her that I wanted to see Tony—that was true. But I'd tell her that we were just friends, and that it was healthy for me to salvage a friendship out of all the confusion he'd caused. "Sure, Mom."

We walked into the kitchen, and I put on water to boil for a cup of tea. At least that gave me a couple of minutes of activity to focus my answers. I got out a mug, an apple cinnamon tea bag, and sugar. Finally I had to sit opposite my mother at the table.

"Cath, I've been doing a lot of thinking about your father, and John and I had a long talk last night."

I'd been wrong again. This wasn't about me after all. Then I stopped to realize that this was about me in a very important way. I pushed Tony out of my mind and focused fully on my mother. "I'm sure you've had a lot to think about, Mom."

"It hasn't been easy. I've been trying to figure out what's best for everyone involved, especially you."

"Mom, you have to figure out what's best for *you*. You can't make yourself miserable trying to do what's best for me, because then I'd be unhappy because you were miserable." I knew what I meant, but I wasn't sure I'd said it clearly. She was looking at me quizzically but then she seemed to sort out the idea.

"That's what I finally decided. Besides, I couldn't figure out what *would* be best for you, other than to provide you with the happiest possible combination of people to live with."

I was getting anxious to hear what she had decided, but I knew better than to rush her.

"John said that he would honor my wishes, whatever they were. If I wanted him to move out, he would. If I wanted to resume a relationship with your father, he would understand."

This didn't surprise me. Mr. Donelly had never struck me as the kind of man who would punch out the competition. He was a nice man, and he certainly wasn't a street brawler.

"However," my mother continued, "I don't want John to leave. He's a healthy part of my life. He respects me and my career, and he treats me as an equal."

"Would Dad ever be able to do that?"

"I'm not sure. He claims that he has changed, and that he knows I'm not the same person I was when he married me, but on an emotional level, I think he still believes that he needs to take care of me."

"Don't you want to be taken care of?"

"On one level, of course I do. It's wonderful to have someone pay the bills and fix the car and make the decisions. On another level, though, that scares me. When you're dependent on someone, you live in fear of losing that person, and I never want to feel like that

144

again. I have proven to myself that I can be in charge of my own life, and I'm not ready to give that up."

"What about Mr. Donelly?"

"One of the things I love about him is that he helps me because he wants to, not because he thinks he has to. He knows that I enjoy his support, but I don't need it. That's an important distinction to me."

There was no doubt what her decision was. "So you're not going to date my father?"

"No, Cath, I'm not. Does that upset you?"

"I understand, Mom. Besides, I really had given up on the fantasy about having some amazing reunion and living happily ever after."

"I'm sorry you had to give up on that. I never intended for our lives to end up like this."

"But they have, Mom, and that's okay, too."

"Thanks, Cath. I hope you know how much guilt you could pile on me if you wanted to."

"I know," I answered with a smile, "and I'm saving it for some future occasion, so watch out."

"I've already talked to your father about this, and he's not happy about it but I think he accepts it. We both agreed that he needs to focus his attention on you."

"Mom," I began, protestingly.

"I know you're angry at him, and you deserve to be, and I told him that. Give him a chance, though. You proved something to him when you walked out of the restaurant. I think he's starting to see you as something other than a child who needs a napkin tucked under her chin."

"That's a relief."

"Are you sure you're okay about all of this?"

"Yes, Mom." And I was. Deep down there was sadness that we'd never be that perfect all-American family with the two kids and the station wagon and the

145

house in the suburbs and the dog named Spot. On the other hand, life with Mom and Mr. Donelly certainly wasn't bad.

"Your water's boiling." Mom's words launched me from the table, and I went to pour my tea. Mr. Donelly stuck his head into the kitchen.

"We need to leave for the office as soon as possible, Angela."

Mom got up, went to him, and rubbed the back of his neck. He looked vaguely embarrassed.

"Are you sure you don't want to come with us later?" Mom asked. "We can stop back when we leave the office and pick you up."

"Thanks, but no." In a way, I was disappointed. I would have loved to see a play, and it would be good to spend time with my mother. Still, seeing Tony was even better.

My mother left the kitchen, Mr. Donelly following her. I sipped my tea and scanned the morning newspaper. I checked the movie listings to see if they'd changed since the night before. They hadn't.

Mom and Mr. Donelly left for the office, and I decided to clean the house first. I put on a Tina Turner tape and danced my way through the living room, dining room, and kitchen. Dust flew, and by the end of the first side, even my bedroom was straightened up. I vacuumed the entire apartment, and for once I didn't even hate that chore. The only thing that slowed me down was that I kept turning off the vacuum every thirty seconds or so to make sure I wasn't missing the phone ringing.

Next I decided to get dressed. I wanted to take a shower, but I knew I'd never hear the phone. I threw on jeans and a sweatshirt, knowing I'd have to change once Tony and I made plans. I even did some homework so there'd be nothing hanging over my head.

A trip to the kitchen to get a glass of Diet Coke created an instant problem—the grocery list. Sure enough, Mom had left a long list on the refrigerator door. Now how was I going to do the shopping without missing Tony's call? I looked at the kitchen clock—9:30. The odds were he wouldn't call quite that early. I dashed to my room, grabbed my Reeboks from under the bed, shoved my feet into them, raced back to kitchen, and grabbed the list and some money out of the flour canister, my mother's hiding place. Then I took the phone off the hook. There. If Tony called and got a busy signal, certainly he'd call back.

The trusty VW bug didn't get a spare moment to warm up, and I turned shopping into an aerobic activity. I was a blur as I raced from aisle to aisle, grabbing the first thing that looked close to what my mother had listed. I scanned the lines intently, searching for the one with the fewest total items in the lineup of carts. I cut off a lady with a cart overflowing with what looked like food for a hundred as I made my move into the checkout line. Luckily I had a cart with four functional wheels; otherwise, that lady would have had tread marks on her legs.

For a moment, I panicked. This was the Acme David worked in. Then I remembered that he had the entire day off. Somehow I had forgotten that he was supposed to call. I pondered that problem as I impatiently waited through the grocery orders in front of me.

Free at last, I hurled the bags into the back seat and headed for home. Rather than make two trips, I juggled three bags at once. I barely made it to the door before one of them began to rip and my arms began to tremble from the weight. I dumped the bags in the hallway as I unlocked the door, then left them there as I raced to put the phone back on the hook. It was only after I had checked three times to make sure the dial tone had resumed that I retrieved the groceries.

All I could hope was that Tony would call before David. Then I could not answer the phone anymore. That would be perfect—no more lies, and David would think that I was with my mother. I figured I was due for a break.

It was almost 11:00 when the phone finally rang. Tony, Tony, Tony, I chanted like a prayer, as if that would control who was there.

"Hello?"

"Cath? This is David."

I wanted to hang up, but I didn't.

"Good morning."

"Did you find out if you'll be home today?"

"I'm sorry, David, but my mother insisted I spend time with my father today." It's a good thing this conversation was over the phone because otherwise David would have been positive I was lying. I hate to lie and I'm bad at it. I could feel my face turning bright red, and I was looking at the floor.

"Well, maybe some other time. Goodbye, Cath."

David sounded sad, and I felt guilty. I knew that I'd feel even worse if I ran into him with Tony. Still, it was a risk I'd have to take. Maybe I could convince Tony to go someplace different where we wouldn't see anyone we knew.

I must admit I also felt some relief. There. David was out of the way. Now all I had to do was wait for Tony's call.

By noon I had given up on the spend the afternoon at the park or the beach theory. By eight, I'd given up on the movie at the mall theory. By ten, I'd given up. I didn't know whether to shout or cry. Why hadn't Tony called? He'd said he would. I'd counted on it. I'd given up Philadelphia and a date with David willingly, but now I felt cheated. Why hadn't he called?

I no longer felt special. I felt ugly and undesirable.

Still, though, maybe he'd call tomorrow. There were lots of things we could do on a Sunday. I tried to hold on to that idea as I sat in the absolute silence of my bedroom.

Chapter Twenty-three

Sunday was a repeat of Saturday, except worse. I never left the apartment; the phone never rang. I hated every minute of it. I despised myself for waiting, but I seemed powerless to do anything else. At one point I had my hand on the doorknob, poised to go out for a walk just to prove to myself that I was free to do what I wanted. I couldn't turn the doorknob, though. I just knew that as soon as I walked out, the phone would ring, and then I would have wasted all the waiting. I couldn't stand it.

I knew Mom was confused. She and Mr. Donelly went out to brunch, and I turned down their invitation to join them. By this time, I knew my mother was getting suspicious, so I told her I didn't feel well. I knew I'd have to make an amazing recovery if Tony actually did call, but I'd worry about that later.

I had nothing to worry about. We didn't even get a wrong number. By the end of the day, I had withdrawn completely into myself. I curled up in a small ball in my bed, head resting on my drawn-up knees. Somehow I figured this must be my fault. Maybe I had misunderstood Tony. Maybe he hadn't meant this weekend. Maybe I had said something to make him change his mind. But what? It must just be that I wasn't interesting enough, pretty enough, special enough to make him want to call.

I hated myself for feeling like that, for once again giving Tony the power to hurt me. I simply couldn't help it, though. I didn't have the energy to fake being anything but miserable, even to myself.

Then I developed a new theory. Maybe something terrible had happened to Tony. Maybe he was sick or in the hospital or dead or something. Then wouldn't I feel terrible for thinking awful things about him? Maybe there was an absolutely valid reason why he hadn't called. Maybe the Ogre had forbidden it, or maybe there was a death in the family. There were thousands of possibilities.

By Monday morning, I wasn't mad at Tony; I was concerned about him. I wanted to know what was wrong. Instead of wanting to avoid him, I went searching for him before homeroom, needing to be sure that he was all right.

I finally found him. Boy, did I find him. His homeroom was on the other side of the building from mine, and I headed in that direction a few minutes before the warning bell was due to ring. As I neared the doorway, I saw him, at least the back of him. He was leaning against a locker, but there was no mistaking his tall, lean build, his slightly curly dark hair. A rush of happiness filled me. At least he was all right. I headed toward him, in fact was only a few feet away, when I saw what his body had been blocking from my view. Also leaning against the lockers, body angled toward Tony's, was Cyndee. She seemed to be gazing adoringly at Tony. I stopped as if an invisible chain had suddenly tethered me, but I couldn't help hearing Tony's words.

"Will you be home tonight? I'll give you a call."

"Probably," came her answer.

"Goodbye, Pretty Girl." Then he touched her hair, pushed it gently back.

He walked away, went into his homeroom. I saw the self-satisfied smile on Cyndee's face before she turned and walked away.

I felt as if I had been physically slapped. It was like watching a movie, except there was a stand-in where I should have been. The same words, the same gesture, the same gentle, caring tone of voice, except the girl wasn't me.

The warning bell jolted me back into the present. I turned and ran through the hallway, back to the relative safety of my homeroom. I wanted to disappear. I wanted to escape from every person, from every male, from Tony.

What a fool I'd been, what an absolute idiot. I had wanted to believe that Tony cared about me so much that I'd convinced myself he'd changed, that I truly did matter to him. It hurt to find out that I was merely one of many, a piece in some game that Tony was playing. And I'd let it happen. I was to blame for believing in fantasies.

The morning was a blur. I sat in classes that I didn't remember, taking out notebooks, opening books, going through the charade. I lived for lunch, when I could talk to Mary. She would know what to say, how to make me understand. She understood males better than I did. Besides, she was my best friend, and I needed her.

The familiar table along the back wall was still our meeting place despite Friday's trauma. More teachers were on duty, standing, prowling, but the cafeteria sounded normal; loud but friendly. I sat in stonefaced silence until Mary finally arrived, slightly breathless. I was in the middle of the whole story about Tony when I noticed that we weren't alone. It was a sign of how immersed I was in my tale that I hadn't heard him come.

152

"Hi," said Mary, looking up. It was Bulldozer Boy. He, of course, did not answer. In fact, he didn't look at Mary at all; he was looking at me. He looked from me down to the chair, and then pulled it out slightly. Obviously he wanted to join us. I couldn't stand it. I needed to talk to Mary, and I couldn't do it with him there.

"Sorry, but these seats are taken." His aqua eyes met mine, and for a moment I glimpsed pure pain. Then his eyes turned off, just as if a switch had been pulled. He whirled away, and I heard muffled shouts as he hurled out of the cafeteria, moving even faster than usual.

Mary was looking at me in surprise. "That wasn't like you, Cath. Aren't you the one who usually lectures me about being nice to people?"

"Did you want him here?" I asked, in a worse mood than ever. All I needed was more guilt.

"No. He gives me the creeps. Does he ever talk?"

"Not that I've ever heard."

"I wonder if he can," Mary said. "Maybe he has some weird disease that has left him unable to speak."

Normally I would have found Mary's questions interesting, but I could still think of nothing but Tony, and I quickly turned the conversation back to that. Mary was sympathetic, which was exactly what I wanted. She wanted me to confront Tony, tell him what a jerk he was, but I knew I couldn't do that. I needed to be mad to do that, and I was mainly sad.

By seventh period, I had calmed down a little, enough to feel bad about Bulldozer Boy. I still hadn't thanked him for all his help on Friday, and now I had rejected him at lunch. I rushed to Spanish class, even though I went by a different route than usual. The last thing I wanted was to pass the Junior Wall and see Tony—or David.

Bulldozer Boy was in his customary seat, his body tense, his eyes darting around the room. I sat down next to him. I could tell he knew l was there, but he didn't look toward me.

"I'm sorry about lunch today," I said quietly. "I was really upset, and I needed to talk to Mary about it. I didn't mean to be rude to you."

There was no response—no eye contact, no acknowledgement. The bell rang, and Mr. Anderson took roll and then began to talk. I opened my notebook and took out a piece of paper. Rapidly I wrote:

I appreciate your help on Friday. I was scared to death in the cafeteria, and I couldn't get out of there. I don't know what I would have done if you hadn't come over. Was it just a coincidence, or did you know I was there?

I shoved the note onto the top of his books, making the gesture obvious so that he'd know what I'd done. He didn't read it. After a few minutes, I took it back and wrote some more:

I don't blame you if you're mad at me for today, but please try to understand that I was in a bad mood and I took it out on you. I'm sorry.

Once again I put the note on his desk. His eyes barely flicked over it, certainly not long enough to read it. Mr. Anderson continued talking about subjunctive verb endings. I felt terrible. I realized that in the whole time I'd known Bulldozer Boy, I'd never seen him make any attempt to join another person, make contact. He was always being laughed at, mocked, pursued, hurt. It must have taken a lot for him to come up to Mary and me, and then I'd rejected him. I felt lower than pond scum.

I'll probably never understand subjunctive verb endings in Spanish. I spent the whole class telling myself what a rotten person I was. Right before the bell rang to end class, Bulldozer Boy began to prepare for his customary dash out the door. He took my note, crumpled it unread into a ball, and threw it on the floor. I guess he told me.

After the bell rang and the room had emptied, I sat there for a minute, trying to gather enough energy to walk out of the building and go home. I just wanted to stay motionless, turn into a rock or a piece of furniture. I felt like a failure, a total, miserable, unloved, unlovable failure. It was only because Mr. Anderson was starting to give me strange looks that I finally gathered my belongings and left.

There, leaning outside the door, was Tony. I couldn't stand it. I couldn't deal with one more thing. I kept walking, not saying a word, but Tony followed me to my locker.

"Sorry I didn't call this weekend. Something came up."

I didn't say anything. Words were floating around in my head, but I didn't have the energy to sort them out.

"I don't blame you for being mad at me, but I did just say I'd try to call, didn't I? It wasn't anything definite."

No, it wasn't, I thought. It was just indefinite enough to make me waste the entire weekend.

Then Tony made his fatal mistake. He leaned close to me, touched my hair, and said gently, "I'll make it up to you, Pretty Girl."

I looked at him as if he'd metamorphosed into a gargoyle. Of course he didn't know I'd overheard his earlier conversation with Cyndee. That's probably why he called us both "Pretty Girl." He was giving the same line to so many that he couldn't keep our names straight. Anger flooded me for the first time, pure, righteous, burning anger.

"Just don't get confused about which Pretty Girl you're talking to at the moment," I said bitterly.

"What do you mean, Catherine?" he said.

"I overheard your touching conversation with Cyndee," I said, not caring if I sounded jealous.

"Oh," Tony said quietly.

"It must be hard to fit all of us into your schedule," I said angrily.

"That's not the way it is," Tony said, anger flaring in his voice, too.

"Isn't it?" I asked.

"With the others, maybe, but not with you."

"Right," I snapped.

"Catherine, the others are just casual, and they play games as much as I do. You're the one who scares me." His voice was soft, and he wouldn't meet my eyes.

"Scares you?" I repeated harshly, thrown by the turn in the conversation, yet wanting to hold on to my anger.

"Yes," he said. "You're the one who made me feel. And I'm afraid to feel too much. I can't handle it. I'm not ready to fall in love, and that's what you made me do."

"Isn't falling in love wonderful?" I asked, confusion filling my mind, sweeping out the anger.

"It is if you're strong enough for it. Catherine, there's something inside me that destroys, and until I get that under control, I can't love anyone, not even myself."

As much as I wanted to argue with him, I knew he was right. "So you're going to bounce from girl to girl, flirting with all of them and caring about none of them?"

"It's the best I can do right now. I won't hurt them; they won't let me."

"And me?" I asked.

"I can't risk destroying you. You're too important to me." The gentleness in his voice was devastating. I believed him, even though I didn't want to.

There was silence between us. I turned and walked away. He started to call after me, but by that point I was running and he didn't follow. Tears had filled my eyes and were running down my face and I didn't want him to see them.

I reached the red VW and threw my books in the back, then slumped in the worn bucket seat of the driver's side. Head on the steering wheel, I sobbed. I cried for myself, for Tony, for my father, for David, for Bulldozer Boy. I cried for all the pain and anger and guilt and realization that filled me to overflowing.

Chapter Twenty-four

It was a time of endings. A few days later, Mary and I were both subdued. Mark was back in school, acting more like a big shot than ever, and I was doing everything I could to avoid Tony. It was another morning that I spent in a daze.

At noon I waited at our lunch table for Mary. I finally saw her weaving her way among the tables, but when she got to me she didn't sit down.

"Library." That was all she said before she headed out again. I followed, wondering what on earth it was this time. The conference room was empty, and once again we evaded the librarian's attention as we shut the door behind us. I waited in silence for Mary to speak, but before she did tears began to stream down her face.

"Mary, what is it?" I grabbed her shoulders and shook her gently. "Tell me."

"I'm not," she whispered.

"You're not what?" I asked before the realization hit me. "You're not pregnant?"

"No." Still Mary cried.

"Mary, are you sure?"

"Positive."

I stared at her in confusion. "Why are you crying? Why aren't you screaming and shouting and jumping with joy?"

"I don't know," she sobbed.

"Aren't you happy you're not pregnant?"

"Yes," she sobbed. She was doing the worst imitation of a happy person I'd seen in a long time. I let her cry.

"Mary," I finally said, "you know how lucky you are, don't you?"

"Yes," she said, and her voice was more controlled. "I feel guilty."

"Why?" I asked.

"I wished and hoped so hard that I wasn't pregnant, that I feel like I killed something."

"Mary, you know that's not true. It just doesn't work that way."

"I know, Cath. And believe me, I know I'm not ready to face all of the responsibility of having a baby. This is wonderful. I'm really happy." Again the tears began to flow.

"Mary, are you sure that there wasn't a little part of you that wanted to have a baby?"

"No," she answered. "I've thought about that, and I'm sure. Besides, what kind of father would Mark be? Fathers shouldn't be cutting class and fighting and getting suspended."

I laughed; I had to. Even Mary smiled.

"Believe me, Cath, I know how lucky I am—and how stupid I was. An hour on Creek Road could have changed my whole life."

"Just remember—no sex for the rest of your life," I reminded her.

"Right," she said. "I never want to go through this again. If I ever get pregnant, I want it to be the exact opposite of this. I want to be wishing and hoping that I *am* pregnant, and then when I am, I want to shout the good news from the rooftops."

"Would you mind waiting a while on that?" I

requested. "I'm not up for another one of these scares either."

Mary looked at me seriously. "How can I thank you, Cath? I would have gone absolutely crazy without you."

"Don't worry about it, Mary. You still went relatively crazy with me."

"You're my best friend," she said.

"I know," I replied, hugging her.

Finally the tension broke, and I could see it in every part of Mary. Her eyes began to glow, and the tension that had become so much a part of her ebbed away. It was as if she truly relaxed for the first time in weeks.

"Let's eat," she said. "What's in your lunch bag?"

I knew the old Mary was back.

Mary's news had made me happy, and I had stopped thinking about Tony. Otherwise, I never would have walked to Spanish by the old route. Before I realized where I was, there was the Junior Wall and the familiar group of guys—and one unwilling addition. They had Bulldozer Boy again.

This time two of the guys had him pinned against the wall, one leaning against each of Bulldozer Boy's shoulders. Tony and David were standing off to the side, watching. Mark was directly in front of Bulldozer Boy. In his hand he had a tennis ball, and he kept bouncing it against the wall right next to Bulldozer Boy's head. I could see Bulldozer Boy straining frantically to get free, but the two guys were leaning their full weight into his shoulders, and he couldn't get loose. It was only when Mark bounced the ball off Bulldozer Boy's forehead that he managed to free one hand. Before Mark could react, Bulldozer Boy snatched the ball. Mark went for it, but it had disappeared into Bulldozer Boy's large hand, his fingers closed over it. It was quick, like a magician's sleight of hand.

"Give me that," snarled Mark.

Suddenly I'd had it. "Leave him alone," I said, pushing up to Mark.

"Stay out of this, Cath," Mark said, not even turning to look at me.

I started to grab Mark's arm, but Tony and David stopped me. They didn't exactly push me, but they moved me back away from Mark, one on either side. I wrenched myself out of Tony's grasp.

"Leave him alone," I said again.

Bulldozer Boy's jacket had come open during his struggle, and I saw Mark stare intently.

"Your shirt says 'Long Hills Tennis Club.' You some kind of tennis player? Or did you steal that shirt?"

Bulldozer Boy met his eyes but said nothing.

"Want to play tennis, Bulldozer Boy?" I heard Mark ask tauntingly. "I bet you'd be real good at that." Some of the rapidly gathering crowd laughed. Bulldozer Boy's refusal to play any sport in gym was well known around school.

I yanked away from David and tried to get back to Mark. Suddenly Bulldozer Boy's eyes met mine, and it was as if I could read his mind. "Don't," his eyes said.

"Want to play?" Mark repeated.

It was in utter amazement that I saw Bulldozer Boy's head nod.

"You do?" said Mark. There was disbelief in his voice.

Again Bulldozer Boy nodded.

"Go ahead, Mark, take him on," I heard a voice shout.

"You'd better not mess with him, Bulldozer Boy. He's ranked third in the state," another voice added. "Nobody in this school can even take a set from him."

Now Mark couldn't back down. "Friday right after school?" he asked.

Bulldozer Boy nodded.

"School courts?" Mark asked.

Again the nod.

"You'd better be there," Mark said. With that Bulldozer Boy pulled free and found a gap and was off. There was silence as we all watched his departure.

Finally Mark laughed. "Can you believe that? He thinks he can play against me." His buddies crowded around, slapping him on the back, joking about placing bets.

I turned around in disgust and walked away.

Bulldozer Boy was already in his seat when I got to Spanish. Even though I once again sat down next to him, he totally ignored me.

"You don't have anything to prove to them," I said quietly. I didn't know whether or not he was listening, but I kept on anyway. "They're immature jerks. Just ignore them."

I realized how unfair that was. After all, that's what Bulldozer Boy had tried to do. He'd tried to just get from class to class in as little time as possible, associate with others as little as possible. He'd ignored everybody in his way—except me, for a while. Now I'd joined the rest of the world.

"I'm sorry. I'm sorry for everything that's happened." The words poured out of me before I could think about them.

Bulldozer Boy's eyes continued to dart around the room, never resting on me. If he had heard me, he didn't give any sign of it.

Chapter Twenty-five

By Friday, the tennis match between Mark and Bulldozer Boy was the talk of the school. You might have thought it was the state championship football game or something. I know one thing for sure—tennis had never gotten that much attention before in the school's history.

I had done my very best to stop it. My talk with Bulldozer Boy had been a failure; he never acknowledged a word I said. Next I had tried Mary.

"Tell Mark to stop this. Tell him to forget the match."

"I tried," Mary said. "I told him that this was going too far, but he's really into it now. So many people have made such a big deal that he couldn't back out now if he wanted to. He also thinks he can't lose."

"Why is Mark behaving like this?" I asked her.

"I honestly don't know," she answered. "It seems like ever since we thought I might be pregnant, he's been acting big and tough. I don't know, maybe it's his way of dealing with tension."

"Well if it is, he should be over it by now. Besides, it isn't fair to make someone else suffer for his bad mood." As soon as I said the words, I realized their hypocrisy. My bad mood had made me reject Bulldozer Boy that day at the lunch table. It seemed like we had all picked the same target.

"I tried, Cath," said Mary, "but I can't get through to Mark anymore. He's almost become a stranger."

I didn't know what else to do. The talk mounted. By Friday, it sounded like half the school would be at the tennis courts to watch the match. In Spanish class, Bulldozer Boy continued to ignore me. I continued to avoid both Tony and David. Everything seemed slightly out of balance.

When the dismissal bell rang on Friday, Bulldozer Boy bolted, and I took my customary walk to my locker. I left the books I didn't need for the weekend, then walked down the hallway to Mary's locker. We had agreed to meet and go to the tennis courts together.

The tennis courts at our school are at the far end of the building between the road that circled the building and the soccer field. There was a slight hill leading to the near edge of the courts, and by the time Mary and I got there, at least thirty people were sitting on the hill, laughing and joking. More were arriving all the time. Mary and I found an open place near the middle with a good view of the whole court, and spread our jackets out to sit on. The weather was amazing—one of those late October warm days that Delaware is occasionally blessed with. Actually it was perfect weather for tennis, just a little brisk but still pleasant.

Up to this point, there wasn't a tennis player in sight, just a crowd of kids yelling to each other, making mocking statements about Bulldozer Boy, betting that he wouldn't even show up. Then the locker room door at the side of the school opened, and Mark walked across the road and down the hill. Tony, David, and a bunch of other guys were around him, escorting him over as if he were the conquering hero. Mark had on navy blue shorts and a plain white tennis shirt. He carried a racquet and a can of balls. As soon as he appeared, the crowd, now at least a hundred strong, began to cheer. Mark bowed, then raised his racquet over his head in acknowledgement. He entered the end court, took the cover off his racquet, and leaned his hands against the fence, first stretching out one leg, then the other. The crowd gave a cheer, accompanied by much laughter. Mark then pulled the tab on the top of the container of balls, and we could hear the hiss of the vacuum being broken. Again, laughter and applause.

Mark looked around in mock bewilderment. "Where's Bulldozer Boy?" he shouted. He shoved two of the balls into the pockets of his shorts, then began to bounce the third one on the court in a show of impatience. I turned away from the court to look around. I didn't know which would be worse—if Bulldozer Boy never appeared, or if he did. I didn't have long to wonder. Around the corner of the building I saw Bulldozer Boy. Inwardly I groaned. He had on that same brown corduroy jacket; that made him even more laughable.

Now a few more people saw him approaching, and they began to chant. "Bulldozer Boy. Bulldozer Boy. Bulldozer Boy." Louder and louder grew the chant, and Mark began to clap in sarcastic approval at the arrival of his opponent.

Bulldozer Boy entered the court, carrying a racquet. He paused at the edge of the playing surface and took off his jacket. Then, to the surprise of the audience, he pulled off the sweatpants he was wearing. Now he was wearing tennis whites, shorts and shirt bearing the logo Long Hills Tennis Club. He had on white Reeboks with small red and blue stripes on the sides and immaculate white tennis socks. He took the cover off his racquet. It was black and gleaming and it looked expensive. The crowd had grown noticeably quieter.

Good for you, I thought. At least you stopped their laughter.

Bulldozer Boy moved to the center of the baseline, racquet balanced in his hands, and looked expectantly at Mark. Mark confidently bounced a ball, then hit it gently over the net. Bulldozer Boy took two quick steps to get into position, then returned the ball. His swing seemed hesitant and stiff, but the ball went back over the net. The two hit the ball back and forth for several minutes, forehands, then backhands, warming up slowly. "Mind if I take a few serves?" Mark finally asked. Bulldozer Boy nodded, then took a position in the right corner of the court. Mark hit several serves, and Bulldozer Boy blocked them back to him.

"I'm ready. Take your practice serves," Mark finally announced. Someone in the crowd cheered, followed by laughter from the rest.

Bulldozer Boy moved just to the right of the service line and hit several serves across court to the left. Two went into the net, and a couple people laughed. Bulldozer Boy hit several from the other side, easy shots that landed in the service block. Then he stopped and looked at Mark and tossed the last ball in his hand over the net to him.

"Best out of three?" Mark asked.

Bulldozer Boy nodded yes.

"Want to serve first?" Mark asked in a rather condescending tone of voice.

Bulldozer Boy shook his head no.

"I'll serve then," announced Mark. The crowd settled expectantly, the buzz of conversation diminishing. The crowd was in a boisterous mood, ready for a good laugh.

Mark served the first ball into the net. The crowd booed him. He laughed, then hit his second serve. It was good, and Bulldozer Boy moved to his right to return it. Mark's return shot went down the left line, and Bulldozer Boy lunged to get it. His shot went out of bounds, and the crowd cheered.

"Fifteen-love," Mark announced.

His next serve was good, and Bulldozer Boy's return went into the net.

"Thirty-love," Mark said.

The third serve was returned solidly by Bulldozer Boy, and the point went on, back and forth. Finally Bulldozer Boy's shot went just a hair long of the baseline.

"Forty-love."

The fourth serve was a beauty on Mark's part. It just got the center service line, and Bulldozer Boy had been playing him toward the alley. He never even got his racquet on it.

"Game," Mark announced. The crowd gave him a resounding cheer. Mark grinned widely, acknowledging the praise.

Bulldozer Boy walked toward the edge of the court, then toward the net. For a moment I thought he was leaving. Then I realized he was changing sides, Mark walking in the opposite direction. I had watched enough matches on television to remember that the players change sides after the odd-numbered games.

It quickly became obvious that Bulldozer Boy wasn't going to announce the score before each serve, as is the custom, so Mark took over that duty. Bulldozer Boy double-faulted on the first point, then hit two balls long. It was love-forty before I knew what had happened. He finally won a point, then lost the next, losing the game fifteen-forty. Again the crowd cheered Mark. I could see Mark's confidence blossoming.

Mark won the next three games easily, in total control. He was always the one on attack, placing the ball so that Bulldozer Boy would have to struggle to get to it. Bulldozer Boy, on the other hand, seemed to be just keeping the ball in play, settling for any shot he could get.

The crowd was getting restless, bored. They had counted on watching Mark slaughter his opponent, and they had counted on being able to laugh at Bulldozer Boy. Well, Mark was winning, but Bulldozer Boy wasn't quite laughable. They didn't know what to do.

It was in the sixth and final game of the first set that I began to notice the change. It was subtle at first, and if I hadn't been watching Bulldozer Boy very carefully I might have missed it. The change first showed up in his serve. Before, he had been merely tapping the ball over the net. In the sixth game, he began to take time over his serve. He bounced the ball several times, staring with rapt attention across the net. He tossed the ball in the air but then caught it rather than hitting it.

"Play ball," someone in the crowd yelled. "Wrong sport, stupid," someone yelled back. "This isn't baseball."

Bulldozer Boy seemed oblivious to the commotion. This time he threw the ball higher and further into the court. It was as if he were watching the ball, calculating his next move. Then he arched his back as his racquet went over his shoulder, and when he hit the ball, his momentum was already carrying him toward the net. The ball rocketed into the service block, and Mark watched it in amazement. He didn't even swing.

Bulldozer Boy moved to serve to the other side, now holding a fifteen-love lead. Again he bounced the ball, threw an experimental toss, then launched another serve. This time Mark got his racquet on the ball, but that was all. The ball arced high and went wide. The score was thirty-love. It was amazing to watch, as if after a slow awakening, Bulldozer Boy's game was coming out of hibernation.

"What's going on?" Mary asked.

"I think he's played this game before," I said.

"He's not going to beat Mark, is he?" Mary asked in consternation.

"Wait and see," I replied, then returned my full attention to the game.

Bulldozer Boy's next few serves were once again easy ones, and Mark again began to win the points. I couldn't figure it out. Why would Bulldozer Boy stop using that hard serve? Before I could come up with a theory, Mark had won the game and the first set, 6–0.

A few people got up off the hill and began to leave. They were satisfied. Life was as it should be. Mark was going to win, and Bulldozer Boy would be in for more mockery.

Mark served to begin the second set. The change in Bulldozer Boy was obvious from the first ball. He began to swing harder, return the ball with much more pace. Now there were times when Mark was the one lunging for the wide ball, racing to the net to cover the short drop shot. For the first time, both players broke a sweat, Mark pausing several times to wipe his palms on his shorts. The first game went to deuce, add in, deuce, add out, deuce again before Mark finally won.

"What's happening?" Mary asked again. I had to explain to her that in tennis if both players get three points, which are scored fifteen, thirty, forty, then it is deuce, or tied. To win the game, one player has to score two points in a row. I'm not sure Mary understood.

"How do you know all of this?" she asked in amazement.

"I love to watch tennis on television," I answered. She looked even more puzzled.

"Watch the match," I told her.

Bulldozer Boy served the second game, and once

again his concentration was back. He paused before each serve, seemed to meditate over each ball, then launched it over the net. The arch in his back, the downward whip of the racquet were graceful, powerful. The force of his serve carried him toward the net, ready to pounce on whatever return of serve Mark managed. The game went to Bulldozer Boy.

Mark held serve the next game, but it was hard. More and more often, Bulldozer Boy attacked the net, coming in to cut off Mark's returns. Now Mark was battling for each point, and Bulldozer Boy was getting stronger and stronger. Even the way he moved changed. He was constantly in motion, darting to left or right, seeming to anticipate where the ball would land before Mark had even hit it. When he was waiting to receive serve, he bounced on his toes, anticipating, poised to react. His concentration was absolute.

The crowd had noticeably quieted down. Even those who knew nothing about tennis could tell that something was happening on the court, something unexpected. Mark was no longer grinning and triumphant; instead, he was starting to look a little worried.

Bulldozer Boy held serve on four straight points, a game that took a matter of minutes. Mark held serve in a battle that went to deuce again and again, finally winning on a shot that barely trickled over the net. Again, Bulldozer Boy easily won his serve, and the set was tied at three all.

It was in the seventh game that Mark began to experience real trouble. If Mark played deep behind the baseline, Bulldozer Boy would drop the ball right over the net. If Mark came in to the net, Bulldozer Boy would lob it deep. Mark was running much more than Bulldozer Boy, and it was beginning to show. Bulldozer Boy broke Mark's serve, then won the next game. He played with such intensity that it was obvious that nothing else existed—just Mark, the tennis ball, and the memories of everything that had been done to him.

Mark served again, and this time I could tell that he was trying to overhit the ball. Desperate to keep the ball out of play, he hit double fault after double fault. When he finally lobbed in some easy serves, Bulldozer Boy was right there to smash them back. That game went to Bulldozer Boy, and the next.

"What does this mean?" Mary asked in a whisper. The crowd was now silent, and any noise seemed sacrilegious in the face of the concentration of the two players.

"It means Bulldozer Boy won the second set 6–3," I told her.

"Is it over?" Mary asked.

"No, they've both won a set now. The third set will decide the match." Inside I was beginning to feel a spreading glow of jubilation. Maybe it wasn't nice to root against Mark, but I was. I thought about him bouncing that tennis ball off the wall next to Bulldozer Boy's head while Bulldozer Boy was pinned by two others.

Bulldozer Boy served the first game of the third set. His concentration seemed total, his reactions quick, his movements graceful. He covered the court effortlessly, always in position to plant his feet and return the ball. Mark, on the other hand, was falling apart. He was pausing more and more often between points, obviously out of breath. He fought valiantly, but now there was a desperation in his game. He lost the first game, then the second one.

During the third game, an amazing thing happened. Mark tried to hit a lob, but it was short. Bulldozer Boy positioned himself under it, then pointed toward the ball with his left hand, spotting it. He raised his racquet, and his overhead smash whizzed the ball past Mark, then kicked high and stuck in the fence. Bulldozer Boy looked loose and confident as he walked back to the baseline.

"All right, Bulldozer Boy," I heard a voice shout.

"Good shot," came another voice.

I could see Mark frown toward the spectators. Bulldozer Boy gave no sign that he had heard anything. He won the game easily. By the end of the fifth game, the crowd was completely behind Bulldozer Boy. They cheered each point, applauded his powerful serves, his overhead smashes. Mark was thoroughly shaken. He was behind in the set 0–5.

Before the sixth and final game, the crowd began to chant, "Bulldozer Boy. Bulldozer Boy. Bulldozer Boy." Suddenly I stood up.

"His name is Robert," I shouted.

Amazingly enough, some of the people heard me over the noise. First a few near me, then more and more changed their chant. "Robert. Robert. Robert." For the first time, I saw a break in Robert's concentration. He looked toward the crowd with a surprised expression on his face. Then he held his hand up, silencing the crowd. Everyone became quiet.

Mark served the game, but he was totally outplayed. No matter what he did, Robert did it better—much better. Mark had lost—game, set, and match. And I didn't feel a bit sorry for him. Grimly he walked to the net, as did Robert. They shook hands, then headed to the sidelines to retrieve racquet covers and clothes.

Mary rushed toward the court and waited at the gate for Mark to walk through. She reached up to hug him, but he pushed her away. Several other guys, Tony, David, surrounded him, and I could hear them saying "Tough match, Mark. Who ever would have thought that Bulldozer Boy could play tennis like that? He'll have to go out for the team this year." Mark shoved angrily away from them and stalked to the locker room door, slamming it shut behind him.

Bulldozer Boy was pulling on his sweatpants, putting the heavy corduroy jacket over his sweaty body. I suddenly realized how he had been able to elude so much of the hallway traffic in school. All of those quick bursts of speed and sudden changes of direction came from tennis.

"You know what, he's actually good-looking," I heard a voice behind me say. It was Cyndee, and she was talking to one of her friends. I had a sudden urge to punch her. Restraining myself, I moved partway down the hill toward the court.

Ten or twenty people were clustered outside the gate now, waiting for Robert. All of his grace and beauty were hidden once more under his jacket, his head again lowered. I could see no celebration in him.

"Great match," one guy called to him.

"Where'd you learn to play like that?" another yelled.

"Will you teach me to play?" Cyndee's flirtatious voice said.

Robert rubbed the surface of his racquet gently and stared at it intently, then straightened a couple of strings. He put it into its cover, and I could hear the zipper closing. He paused for a moment and looked at the gang of people clustered at the gate. Then he walked toward them and through them, saying nothing, stopping for none of them. They followed him, but he continued to ignore them and eventually they stopped.

I was partway down the hill, alone now. Bulldozer Boy headed straight for me. I thought he was going to walk right past, but when he was an arm's length away, he stopped.

His eyes met mine, eyes full of sadness and pain.

He looked at me, and it was as if all the sorrow in the world was radiating out of him and into me. I wanted to touch him, to hold him, to comfort him, but I knew I couldn't. As if reading my mind, he shook his head slightly.

"Goodbye," he said in a whisper.

At first I wasn't sure if he had actually spoken, or if I had read the word in his eyes. The word echoed in my mind, however, and I knew that he had said it.

"Wait," I called, but he was already gone.

Chapter Twenty-six

I had to know. All weekend I thought about Robert, and I had come up with no answers. I wanted to talk to him, needed to talk to him, even if he wouldn't answer me. I had to have the chance to apologize again, for myself, for all of us. I needed to tell him not to hate us, even though he deserved to.

I searched for him desperately on Monday even as I knew he wouldn't be there. I knew that he wouldn't have said goodbye unless he meant it, but I hoped against hope that he had changed his mind. His tennis had won him acceptance, but what would that mean to him? Why should he want the acceptance of any of us?

I rushed to seventh-period Spanish class, desperate for the sight of his brown corduroy jacket in the back corner. It was empty. I almost cried.

I needed answers, so after the final bell rang I went up to Mr. Anderson. After all, he had gotten me into this by pairing me with Bulldozer Boy. He was sitting at his desk, pen in hand, staring intently at whatever paper he was grading.

"Mr. Anderson?" I said hesitantly.

He looked up in surprise, his concentration broken, but then he smiled. "Yes?" he said.

"Mr. Anderson, I need help."

"What kind of help, Cath?"

I guess he could tell that it wasn't easy for me to ask, so he waited patiently.

"I need to know about Robert Sullivan, Mr. Anderson." Then the whole story poured out, how the kids had tormented him, how he'd never fought back, how he had beaten Mark at tennis. I even admitted that I had rejected him at lunch and added to all of his pain. Mr. Anderson listened in silence.

"You say that through all of this, he never spoke?" he finally asked.

"He can speak," I said.

"How do you know that?"

"He said goodbye to me after the tennis match."

Tears welled up in my eyes, and Mr. Anderson came from behind his desk to sit next to me. He patted my shoulder.

"Cath, don't be too hard on yourself. You were nicer to him than anyone else in the building, and he knew that. That's why he chose you to speak to. That's a great compliment."

"Why, Mr. Anderson? Why would someone choose to never speak? Why did he race through the halls and give everyone the ammunition to make fun of him?"

"You really need to know, don't you?"

"Yes," I said quietly. "Yes."

"You are right, Cath. There is quite a reason behind his behavior."

"Please tell me." I couldn't have stood to get this close to solving the mystery and then to have the clues withheld.

"You know the information is confidential, don't you? I'm trusting you, Cath." Mr. Anderson looked tense and sad.

"I know," I said, not sure that I deserved anyone's trust.

"According to the records, Robert Sullivan transferred here from Long Hills Academy, a private school in Ridgefield, Connecticut.''

That made sense. The logo on his tennis clothes had been Long Hills Tennis Club.

"He was an honors student through ninth grade, straight A's, in fact,'' continued Mr. Anderson.

That also made sense. He certainly was a good Spanish student.

"During August of the summer between his ninth and tenth grade years, his father was shot. Evidently Robert witnessed the murder. They've never caught the murderer. Apparently the police don't think they'll ever solve the murder after this much time.''

I felt like I couldn't breathe. No wonder he wouldn't trust people.

"Robert spent last year in a private juvenile psychiatric unit. He hadn't said a word since his father's death.''

Until he spoke to me? My God.

"The report from the chief psychiatrist there indicated that Robert posed no threat to others or to himself. Her recommendation was that Robert be returned to a school setting where he could start fresh, without the notoriety of his father's murder. She believed that his superior intelligence would allow him to succeed academically, and that eventually his antisocial behavior would decrease as he won acceptance from his peers. She believed that then he would resume speaking.''

"Why did he end up here?" I asked.

"His mother died when he was an infant, and after his father's death the court awarded custody to his only living relative, an aunt who lives here in Delaware.''

"What is her name?"

"Cath, you're really putting me on the spot. I shouldn't be telling you all this.''

"If you don't tell me, I'll find out some other way."

"You will, won't you?" said Mr. Anderson. "Her name is Elizabeth Maguire."

"Why, Mr. Anderson? Why couldn't we just let him be? Why did people have to trip him and punch him and torment him? Why didn't we try to find out why he acted the way he did, rather than being so quick to laugh at him?"

"Cath, adolescence is a rough time."

"But does it have to be so cruel?"

"For some, I guess it does. If they're insecure, not confident of their own worth, they're fast to find someone weaker, someone alone and vulnerable to attack, to laugh at. They try to make themselves bigger by diminishing someone else."

"But that's not fair," I protested.

"Whoever said high school is fair?" Mr. Anderson said gently.

"Why do you stay here?" I asked. At the moment, I wanted to be as far away from high school as I could get.

"Because I understand, and because sometimes I think I can help."

"Am I as bad as all the rest?" I asked. "Did I hurt Robert worse than all the others?"

"No, Cath. You did the best you could. He knew that you were different. You broke through his shell more successfully than anyone else here, and that's because he knew you were willing to try to accept him as he was."

"But he shut me out again."

"Sure he did, but not all the way. Do you realize how difficult it must have been for him to break a year of silence? You did that. A terrible person wouldn't have achieved that."

"I have to find him, Mr. Anderson. I have to ask

him to give me another chance, to let me do better this time.''

"I hope you do find him, Cath. He's lucky if you do.''

Mr. Anderson's words touched me. "Thank you," I said. "I'll let you know what happens.''

"You'd better," he said with a smile. "Good luck.''

I walked to the door and was ready to leave when Mr. Anderson's voice stopped me.

"Try not to be too hard on yourself, Cath. You've got a good and giving heart. I sensed that the day I paired you with Robert.''

I tried to smile.

I headed straight for the school lobby where I knew there was a phone and, hopefully, a phone book. Luckily the M section hadn't been ripped out, and I found a listing for Maguire, E. L. The address was a street whose name I vaguely recognized. I started to search for a quarter to call, then changed my mind. Maybe I'd do better in person.

I dashed to the parking lot, started the VW, and began my search. It took stops at two gas stations before I found someone who could give me directions, but finally I was parked in front of a medium-sized ranch house. Children's bikes were thrown in the front yard, and what had once been Christmas lights dangled from the branches of a large maple tree.

I went to the front door and knocked hesitantly. Eventually it was opened by a large woman who looked very tired. I could hear an afternoon soap opera blaring in the background, accompanied by the arguing voices of several young children.

"Mrs. Maguire?" I asked politely.

"Yes," she said. "Can I help you?''

"May I please speak to Robert?''

"I wish you could," she said.

"I just need to see him for a moment," I said. "I'm a friend of his from school."

"Friend? I'm so glad that Robert finally found a friend." She seemed genuinely moved.

"Please, Mrs. Maguire, will you tell him that Cath Berry is here?"

"I'm afraid I can't do that," she replied. "I haven't seen him in days."

Since Friday, I supposed. "Do you know where he is?" I asked, knowing I was pushing my luck.

"I wish I did. I've got five kids of my own to keep track of, but I've done my very best to make Robert feel welcome. My heart nearly broke when those court people told me he had nowhere else to live. My sister has been dead for sixteen years, but that would never stop me from trying to love her son."

"Have you let anyone know that he's missing?"

"I've called the social worker who's supposed to check on him. I'm just praying he'll show up again any minute."

"If he does, will you tell him that Cath Berry wants to see him?"

"Sure, honey. Thank you for caring and taking the time to stop by." With that, she shut the door.

I wasn't about to give up my search. Maybe I could figure out where he might have gone if I knew more about his past. Suddenly I had a new theory.

The University of Delaware library is a huge building faced with red brick. I'd been there several times to do research for school projects and had found it mind-boggling. Still, I knew that they had newspaper files. One of my history teachers had made us research what had happened on the day we were born, and I had learned how to use the microfilm files.

I found a parking space, which was a miracle in that vicinity, and headed for the library basement. There was a listing of the newspapers for which the library kept files, and I found a code for the *Ridgefield Sentinel* in Connecticut. Mr. Anderson had said that Robert's father had been killed during the summer between ninth and tenth grades. I went to the file drawer and started back sixteen months.

The first time I put the microfilm in the viewer it was upside down and out of focus, but eventually I got it in right. I started in June, my head getting dizzy as I quickly scanned to find the front page of each day's paper. It wasn't until I got to August 5 that I found what I was looking for. There was the headline in boldface type: "Local Tennis Pro Brendan Sullivan Murdered."

I read the article, my hands shaking. It was all starting to make sense. Robert's father had been the head pro at the Long Hills Tennis Club. Evidently he had also played in a lot of tournaments and was the highest ranking player in Connecticut in the thirty-five and over age group. The newspaper reporter had interviewed several members of the club, all of whom raved about what an enthusiastic teacher and coach Brendan was.

Then there were the pictures. Brendan Sullivan had the same thick hair, the same stocky build as Robert. I couldn't tell if his eyes were aqua, but I bet they were. He was a handsome man with a ready grin, and I could see exactly what Robert would look like if he were happy and relaxed. Then I saw the picture of father and son. Robert looked to be maybe ten or eleven, and the caption read, "Brendan Sullivan and son Robert after winning the state father-son tournament." Robert was looking up at his father adoringly, smiling at him rather than at the large trophy he was holding.

Then came the gory details. Brendan had organized

a tournament for young players at the club, and the competition had continued until about nine o'clock at night. All of the players and parents had left, and Brendan and Robert had stayed to collect the balls, loosen the nets, lock up the courts, and turn out the large lights that lit the playing area. As nearly as the police could tell, Brendan and Robert had been walking from the courts to the parking lot when someone had stepped out from the darkness and shot Brendan Sullivan in the back at point-blank range.

A passing motorist called the police after hearing Robert's screams. When the first squad car arrived, they found Robert cradling the bloody body of his already dead father.

According to the newspaper account, the boy was in shock and could provide no details about his father's attacker.

Day after day, the front page stories reported no progress in finding the murderer of Brendan Sullivan. Robert was reported to be under medical care, and the police doubted that he would be able to provide a description due to the darkness. Reporters conducted interview after interview. No one seemed to believe that Brendan Sullivan had any enemies. One person speculated that the murderer was the jealous husband of one of his tennis students; others believed that the killer had picked a random victim. The bottom line was that no one knew.

By September, the story barely made the paper. Occasionally there would be a report that the police were still searching for clues that would help solve the case, and eventually the Long Hills Tennis Club members raised $10,000 to be given to anyone providing information that would lead to the capture and conviction of the murderer of Brendan Sullivan. It seemed the money was never claimed.

I returned the microfilm to its drawer and walked out of the library. The pieces were all starting to fit together. No wonder Robert rushed through the halls, not wanting anyone near him. No wonder he would only sit in the back corner. His father had been killed from behind, and now he could barely tolerate anyone behind him. No wonder he could play tennis with such skill and grace, but no wonder it had taken such cruel taunting to drive him to play it again. What memories tennis had to hold for him, memories too painful to face.

Robert had tried to leave his past behind, but it had followed him.

Chapter Twenty-seven

I haven't found Robert Sullivan yet, but I will. I have a list of possibilities. I'm going to call Elizabeth Maguire again and see if he has come back. Somehow I doubt that he has, but it's a chance. I'm also going to see if she'll give me the name of Robert's social worker. If she won't, I'll see if Mr. Anderson can find it in the school records. If he can't, I'll call the Bureau of Child Protection and start asking.

I also called Information for the phone number of the Long Hills Tennis Club. Then I called there, got the address, and wrote to the manager to see if he could put me in touch with anyone who knew Robert. I'll write to the newspaper, the police department, to the private school Robert used to attend, to his psychiatrist. I'll beg them to try to find him, and if they do, I'll beg them to give him my address and ask him to write to me. It's worth a chance. It's the only chance I have.

I need to see him. I need to try to convince Robert that he owes it to himself to give people—to give me— one more chance. I need to prove to him that I'm not like the rest. I need to tell him about Mr. Anderson's theory. Kids are cruel because they don't like who they are yet. They're doing the best they can, even if that isn't very good sometimes.

I need to feel at peace with myself again, and to do that I need to find Robert.

He deserves to know what he's taught me. He needs to know that because of him, I'll always try to see beyond the surface and into whatever it is that causes a person to be what he is. I'll try not to underestimate the pain that lives behind the eyes.

I know that Mary will be okay, with or without Mark. I understand Tony now, even though what I've learned makes me sad. Maybe I'll try to be nicer to David, take the time to find out what's inside him. Even my Dad—he's struggling, too, doing the best he can at a difficult time in his life. He's not perfect, but I can't expect him to be.

All I need is to find Robert, to show him—and myself—that I'm doing the best I can, too. I wish we could start over, and maybe this time I'd give him the chance to say more than goodbye.

JANE McFANN lives in Newark, Delaware. She teaches English at Glasgow High School, where her students provide much of the inspiration for her writing. When she is not teaching or writing, her interests include tennis, music, and tormenting her friends by threatening to put them in her next book. ONE MORE CHANCE is her second novel; it is the sequel to *Maybe By Then I'll Understand*. She is presently at work on a new book.